THE MAGNIFICENT BESTSELLING
AMBER SERIES
BY HUGO AND NEBULA AWARD
WINNER

ROGER ZELAZNY

NINE PRINCES IN AMBER
THE GUNS OF AVALON
SIGN OF THE UNICORN
THE HAND OF OBERON
THE COURTS OF CHAOS

"I GENUINELY ENVY THOSE WHO EN-
COUNTER ROGER ZELAZNY!"
—Theodore Sturgeon, *The New York Times*

"DARING AND MAGNIFICENT. THIS IS WHAT
SCIENCE FICTION IS FOR...MAY ZELAZNY
PURSUE HIS QUEST IN THE AMBER BOOKS
TO COME."
Magazine of Fantasy and Science Fiction

"ZELAZNY IS ONE OF SF'S BRIGHTEST
LIGHTS...His worlds are imaginative, his plots
tightly presented, and his characters believably
alive."
Library Journal

Avon Books by
Roger Zelazny

CREATURES OF LIGHT AND DARKNESS
DOORWAYS IN THE SAND
LORD OF LIGHT

The Amber novels

NINE PRINCES IN AMBER
THE GUNS OF AVALON
SIGN OF THE UNICORN
THE HAND OF OBERON
THE COURTS OF CHAOS
TRUMPS OF DOOM

TRUMPS OF DOOM

AVON
PUBLISHERS OF BARD, CAMELOT, DISCUS AND FLARE BOOKS

AVON BOOKS
A division of
The Hearst Corporation
1790 Broadway
New York, New York 10019

Copyright © 1985 by The Amber Corporation
Published by arrangement with the author
Library of Congress Catalog Card Number: 84-29776
ISBN: 0-380-89635-4
Cover illustration by Tim White

The Arbor House edition contains the following Library of Congress Cata-
loging in Publication Data:

Zelazny, Roger.
    Trumps of doom.

    I. Title.
PS3576.E43T7   1985   813'.54   84-29776

First Avon Printing, February 1986

Printed in the U. S. A.

K-R 10 9 8 7 6 5 4 3 2

Again, Judy

TRUMPS OF
DOOM

CHAPTER 1

It is a pain in the ass waiting around for someone to try to kill you. But it was April 30, and of course it would happen as it always did. It had taken me a while to catch on, but now I at least knew when it was coming. In the past, I'd been too busy to do anything about it. But my job was finished now. I'd only stayed around for this. I felt that I really ought to clear the matter up before I departed.

I got out of bed, visited the bathroom, showered, brushed my teeth, et cetera. I'd grown a beard again, so I didn't have to shave. I was not jangling with strange apprehensions, as I had been on that April 30 three years ago when I'd awakened with a headache and a premonition, thrown open the windows, and gone to the kitchen to discover all of the gas burners turned on and flameless. No. It wasn't even like the April 30 two years ago in the other apartment when I awoke before dawn to a faint smell of smoke to learn that the place was on fire. Still, I stayed out of direct line of the light fixtures in case the bulbs were filled with something flammable, and I flipped all of the switches rather than pushing them. Nothing untoward followed these actions.

1

Usually, I set up the coffee maker the night before with a timer. This morning, though, I didn't want coffee that had been produced out of my sight. I set a fresh pot going and checked my packing while I waited for it to brew. Everything I valued in this place resided in two medium-sized crates—clothing, books, paintings, some instruments, a few souvenirs, and so forth. I sealed the cases. A change of clothing, a sweatshirt, a good paperback, and a wad of traveler's checks went into the backpack. I'd drop my key off at the manager's on the way out, so he could let the movers in. The crates would go into storage.

No jogging for me this morning.

As I sipped my coffee, passing from window to window and pausing beside each for sidelong surveys of the streets below and the buildings across the way (last year's attempt had been by someone with a rifle), I thought back to the first time it had happened, seven years ago. I had simply been walking down the street on a bright spring afternoon when an oncoming truck had swerved, jumped the curb, and nearly combined me with portions of a brick wall. I was able to dive out of the way and roll. The driver never regained consciousness. It had seemed one of those freak occurrences that occasionally invade the lives of us all.

The following year to the day, however, I was walking home from my lady friend's place late in the evening when three men attacked me—one with a knife, the other two with lengths of pipe—without even the courtesy of first asking for my wallet.

I left the remains in the doorway of a nearby record store, and while I thought about it on the way home it did not strike me until the following day that it had been the anniversary of the truck crash. Even then, I dismissed it as an odd coincidence. The matter of the mail bomb that had destroyed half of another apartment the following year did cause me to begin wondering whether the statistical nature of reality might not be under a strain in my vicinity at that season. And the events of subsequent years served to turn this into a conviction.

Someone enjoyed trying to kill me once a year, it was as simple as that. The effort failing, there would be another year's pause before an attempt was made again. It seemed almost a game.

But this year I wanted to play, too. My main concern was that he, she, or it seemed never to be present when the event occurred, favoring stealth and gimmicks or agents. I will refer to this person as S (which sometimes stands for "sneak" and sometimes for "shithead" in my private cosmology), because X has been overworked and because I do not like to screw around with pronouns with disputable antecedents.

I rinsed my coffee cup and the pot and set them in the rack. Then I picked up my bag and departed. Mr. Mulligan wasn't in, or was sleeping, so I left my key in his mailbox before heading up the street to take my breakfast at a nearby diner.

Traffic was light, and all of the vehicles well behaved. I walked slowly, listening and looking. It was a pleasant morning, promising a beautiful day. I hoped to settle things quickly, so I could enjoy it at my leisure.

I reached the diner unmolested. I took a seat beside the window. Just as the waiter came to take my order I saw a familiar figure swinging along the street—a former classmate and later fellow employee—Lucas Raynard: six feet tall, red-haired, handsome in spite, or perhaps because, of an artistically broken nose, with the voice and manner of the salesman he was.

I knocked on the window and he saw me, waved, turned and entered.

"Merle, I was right," he said, coming up to the table, clasping my shoulder briefly, seating himself and taking the menu out of my hands. "Missed you at your place and guessed you might be here."

He lowered his eyes and began reading the menu.

"Why?" I asked.

"If you need more time to consider, I'll come back," the waiter said.

"No," Luke answered and read off an enormous order. I added my own. Then: "Because you're a creature of habit."

"Habit?" I replied. "I hardly eat here anymore."

"I know," he answered, "but you usually did when the pressure was on. Like, right before exams—or if something was bothering you."

"Hm," I said. There did seem to be something to that, though I had never before realized it. I spun the ashtray with its imprint of a unicorn's head, a smaller version of the stained-glass one that stood as part of a partition beside the doorway. "I can't say why," I finally stated. "Besides, what makes you think something's bothering me?"

"I remembered that paranoid thing you have about April 30, because of a couple of accidents."

"More than a couple. I never told you about all of them."

"So you still believe it?"

"Yes."

He shrugged. The waiter came by and filled our coffee cups.

"Okay," he finally agreed. "Have you had it yet today?"

"No."

"Too bad. I hope it doesn't pall your thinking."

I took a sip of coffee.

"No problem," I told him.

"Good." He sighed and stretched. "Listen, I just got back to town yesterday . . ."

"Have a good trip?"

"Set a new sales record."

"Great."

"Anyhow . . . I just learned when I checked in that you'd left."

"Yeah. I quit about a month ago."

"Miller's been trying to reach you. But with your phone disconnected he couldn't call. He even stopped by a couple of times, but you were out."

"Too bad."

"He wants you back."

"I'm finished there."

"Wait'll you hear the proposition, huh? Brady gets kicked upstairs and you're the new head of Design—for a twenty percent pay hike. That's what he told me to tell you."

I chuckled softly.

"Actually, it doesn't sound bad at all. But, like I said, I'm finished."

"Oh." His eyes glistened as he gave me a sly smile. "You *do* have something lined up someplace else. He was wondering. Okay, if that's the case he told me to tell you to bring him whatever the other guys offered. He'll try like hell to top it."

I shook my head.

"I guess I'm not getting through," I said. "I'm finished. Period. I don't want to go back. I'm not going to work for anyone else either. I'm done with this sort of thing. I'm tired of computers."

"But you're really good. Say, you going to teach?"

"Nope."

"Well, hell! You've got to do something. Did you come into some money?"

"No. I believe I'll do some traveling. I've been in one place too long."

He raised his coffee cup and drained it. Then he leaned back, clasped his hands across his stomach, and lowered his eyelids slightly. He was silent for a time.

Finally: "You said you were finished. Did you just mean the job and your life here, or something else as well?"

"I don't follow you."

"You had a way of disappearing—back in college, too. You'd be gone for a while and then just as suddenly turn up again. You always were vague about it, too. Seemed like you were leading some sort of double life. That have anything to do with it?"

"I don't know what you mean."

He smiled.

"Sure you do," he said. When I did not reply, he added, "Well, good luck with it—whatever."

Always moving, seldom at rest, he fidgeted with a key

ring while we had a second cup of coffee, bouncing and jangling keys and a blue stone pendant. Our breakfasts finally arrived and we ate in silence for a while.

Then he asked, "You still have the *Starburst?*"

"No. Sold her last fall," I told him. "I'd been so busy I just didn't have time to sail. Hated to see her idle."

He nodded.

"That's too bad," he said. "We had a lot of fun with her, back in school. Later, too. I'd have liked to take her out once more, for old times' sake."

"Yes."

"Say, you haven't seen Julia recently."

"No, not since we broke up. I think she's still going with some guy named Rick. Have you?"

"Yeah. I stopped by last night."

"Why?"

He shrugged.

"She was one of the gang—and we've all been drifting apart."

"How was she?"

"Still looking good. She asked about you. Gave me this to give to you, too."

He withdrew a sealed envelope from inside his jacket and passed it to me. It bore my name, in her handwriting. I tore it open and read:

Merle,
I was wrong. I know who you are and there is danger.
I have to see you. I have something you will need. It
is very important. Please call or come by as soon as
you can.
Love,

Julia

"Thanks," I said, opening my pack and filing it.

It was puzzling as well as unsettling. In the extreme. I'd have to decide what to do about it later. I still liked her more than I cared to think about, but I wasn't sure I wanted to see her again. But what did she mean about knowing who I am?

I pushed her out of my mind, again.

I watched the traffic for a time and drank coffee and thought about how I'd first met Luke, in our freshman year, in the Fencing Club. He was unbelievably good.

"Still fence?" I asked him.

"Sometimes. How about you?"

"Occasionally."

"We never really did find out who was better."

"No time now," I said.

He chuckled and poked his knife at me a few times.

"I guess not. When are you leaving?"

"Probably tomorrow—I'm just cleaning up a few odds and ends. When that's done I'll go."

"Where are you heading?"

"Here and there. Haven't decided on everything yet."

"You're crazy."

"Um-hm. *Wanderjahr* is what they used to call it. I missed out on mine and I want it now."

"Actually it does sound pretty nice. Maybe I ought to try it myself sometime."

"Maybe so. I thought you took yours in installments, though."

"What do you mean?"

"I wasn't the only one who used to take off a lot."

"Oh, that." He dismissed it with the wave of a hand. "That was business, not pleasure. Had to do some deals to pay the bills. You going to see your folks?"

Strange question. Neither of us had ever spoken of our parents before, except in the most general terms.

"I don't think so," I said. "How're yours?"

He caught my gaze and held it, his chronic smile widening slightly.

"Hard to say," he replied. "We're kind of out of touch."

I smiled, too.

"I know the feeling."

We finished our food, had a final coffee.

"So you won't be talking to Miller?" he asked.

"No."

He shrugged again. The check came by and he picked it up.

"This one's on me," he said. "After all, I'm working."

"Thanks. Maybe I can get back at you for dinner. Where're you staying?"

"Wait." He reached into his shirt pocket, took out a matchbook, tossed it to me. "There. New Line Motel," he said.

"Say I come by about six?"

"Okay."

He settled up and we parted on the street.

"See you," he said.

"Yeah."

Bye-bye, Luke Raynard. Strange man. We'd known each other for almost eight years. Had some good times. Competed in a number of sports. Used to jog together almost every day. We'd both been on the track team. Dated the same girls sometimes. I wondered about him again—strong, smart, and as private a person as myself. There was a bond between us, one that I didn't fully understand.

I walked back to my apartment's parking lot and checked under my car's hood and frame before I tossed my pack inside and started the engine. I drove slowly, looking at things that had been fresh and new eight years before, saying good-bye to them now. During the past week I had said it to all of the people who had mattered to me. Except for Julia.

It was one of those things I felt like putting off, but there was no time. It was either now or not at all, and my curiosity had been piqued. I pulled into a shopping mall's lot and located a pay phone, but there was no answer when I rang her number. I supposed she could be working full-time on a dayshift again, but she could also be taking a shower or be out shopping. I decided to drive on over to her place and see. It wasn't that far. And whatever it was that she had for me, picking it up would be a good excuse for seeing her this one last time.

I cruised the neighborhood for several minutes before I located a parking space. I locked the car, walked back to the corner, and turned right. The day had grown slightly warmer. Somewhere, dogs were barking.

I strolled on up the block to that huge Victorian house that had been converted into apartments. I couldn't see her windows from the front. She was on the top floor, to the rear. I tried to suppress memories as I passed on up the front walk, but it was no good. Thoughts of our times together came rushing back along with a gang of old feelings. I halted. It was silly coming here. Why bother, for something I hadn't even missed. Still . . .

Hell. I *wanted* to see her one more time. I wasn't going to back out now. I mounted the steps and crossed the porch. The door was open a crack so I walked in.

Same foyer. Same tired-looking potted violet, dust on its leaves, on the chest before the gilt-framed mirror——the mirror that had reflected our embrace, slightly warped, many times. My face rippled as I went by.

I climbed the green-carpeted stairs. A dog began howling somewhere out back.

The first landing was unchanged. I walked the short hallway, past the drab etchings and the old end table, turned and mounted the second staircase. Halfway up I heard a scratching noise from overhead and a sound like a bottle or a vase rolling on a hardwood floor. Then silence again, save for a few gusts of wind about the eaves. A faint apprehension stirred within me and I quickened my pace. I halted at the head of the stairway and nothing looked to be out of order, but with my next inhalation a peculiar odor came to me. I couldn't place it—sweat, must, damp dirt perhaps—certainly something organic.

I moved then to Julia's door and waited for several moments. The odor seemed stronger there, but I heard no new sounds.

I rapped softly on the dark wood. For a moment it seemed

that I heard someone stirring within, but only for a moment.
I knocked again.

"Julia?" I called out. "It's me—Merle."

Nothing. I knocked louder.

Something fell with a crash. I tried the doorknob. Locked.

I twisted and jerked and tore the doorknob, the lock plate,
and the entire locking mechanism free. I moved immediately
to my left then, past the hinged edge of the door and the
frame. I extended my left hand and applied gentle pressure
to the upper panel with my fingertips.

I moved the door a few inches inward and paused. No
new sounds ensued, and nothing but a slice of wall and
floor came into view, with narrow glimpses of a watercolor,
the red sofa, the green rug. I eased the door open a little
farther. More of the same. And the odor was even stronger.

I took a half-step to my right and applied a steady pressure.

Nothingnothingnothing . . .

I snatched my hand away when she came into view. Lying
there. Across the room. Bloody . . .

There was blood on the floor, the rug, a bloody disarray
near the corner off to my left. Upset furniture, torn cushions . . .

I suppressed an impulse to rush forward.

I took one slow step and then another, all of my senses
alert. I crossed the threshold. There was nothing else/no
one else in the room. Frakir tightened about my wrist. I
should have said something then, but my mind was elsewhere.

I approached and knelt at her side. I felt sick. From the
doorway I had not been able to see that half of her face and
her right arm were missing. She was not breathing and her
carotid was silent. She had on a torn and bloodied peach-
colored robe; there was a blue pendant about her neck.

The blood that had spilled beyond the rug onto the hardwood floor was smeared and tracked. They were not human
footprints, however, but large, elongated, three-toed things,
well padded, clawed.

A draft of which I had been only half-consciously aware—coming from the opened bedroom door at my back—was suddenly diminished, as the odor intensified. There came another quick pulsing at my wrist. There was no sound, though. It was absolutely silent, but I knew that it was there.

I spun up out of my kneeling position into a crouch, turning—

I saw a large mouthful of big teeth, bloody lips curled back around them. They lined the muzzle belonging to several hundred pounds of doglike creature covered with coarse, moldy-looking yellow fur. Its ears were like clumps of fungi, its yellow-orange eyes wide and feral.

As I had no doubt whatever concerning its intentions I hurled the doorknob, which I had been clutching half-consciously for the past minute. It glanced off the bony ridge above its left eye without noticeable effect. Still soundless, the thing sprang at me.

Not even time for a word to Frakir . . .

People who work in slaughterhouses know that there is a spot on an animal's forehead to be found by drawing an imaginary line from the right ear to the left eye and another from the left ear to the right eye. They aim the killing blow an inch or two above the junction of this X. My uncle taught me that. He didn't work in a slaughterhouse, though. He just knew how to kill things.

So I spun forward and to the side as it sprang, and I struck a hammer blow at the death spot. It moved even faster than I'd anticipated, however, and when my fist struck it, it was already rushing by. Its neck muscles helped it to absorb the force of my blow.

This drew the first sound from it, though—a yelp. It shook its head and turned with great speed then, and it was at me again. Now a low, rumbling growl came up from its chest and its leap was high. I knew that I was not going to be able to sidestep this one.

My uncle had also taught me how to grab a dog by the flesh on the sides of its neck and under the jaws. You need a good grip if it's a big one, and you've got to get it just right. I had no real choice at the moment. If I tried a kick and missed it would probably take off my foot.

My hands shot forward and snaked upward and I braced myself when we met. I was sure it outweighed me and I had to meet its momentum as well.

I'd had visions of losing fingers or a hand, but I got in under the jaw, caught hold and squeezed. I kept my arms extended and leaned into the impact. I was shaken by the force of its lunge, but I was able to maintain my grip and absorb it.

As I listened to the growls and regarded the slavering muzzle a foot or so away from my face I realized that I hadn't thought much beyond this point. With a dog, you might be able to bash its head against anything hard and handy; its carotids are too deeply buried to rely on direct pressure to take it out. But this thing was strong and my grip was already beginning to slip against its frantic twisting. As I held its jaws away from me and kept pushing it upward, I also realized that it was taller than I was when extended along the vertical. I could try for a kick at its soft underside, but I would probably go off balance as well as lose my grip, and then my groin would be exposed to its teeth.

But it twisted free of my left hand, and I had no choice but to use my right or lose it. So I pushed as hard as I could and retreated again. I had been looking for a weapon, any weapon, but there was nothing handy that would serve.

It lunged again, coming for my throat, coming too fast and high for me to manage a kick to its head. I couldn't get out of its way either.

Its forelegs were level with my midriff, and I hoped that my uncle had been right about this one too, as I seized them and twisted backward and inward with all of my strength, dropping to one knee to avoid those jaws, chin lowered to protect my throat, my head drawn back. Bones popped and crunched as I twisted and its head lowered almost immediately to attack my wrists. But by then I was already rising, thrusting forward, springing up.

It went over backward, twisted, and almost caught itself.

When its paws struck the floor, however, it made a sound halfway between a whimper and a snarl and collapsed forward.

I was about to try for another blow to the skull when it recovered its footing, moving faster than I'd thought it could. It raised its right foreleg immediately upon standing and balanced itself on three legs, still growling, eyes fixed on my own, saliva dampening its lower jaw. I moved slightly to my left, certain that it was about to rush me yet again, angling my body, positioning myself in a way that no one had taught me, because I do occasionally have original thoughts.

It was a little slower when it came for me this time. Maybe I could have gone for the skull and gotten it. I don't know because I didn't try. I seized it once more by the neck, and this time it was familiar territory. It would not pull away as it had before in the few moments I needed. Without breaking its momentum I turned and dropped low and thrust and pulled, adding some guidance to its trajectory.

It turned in midair, its back striking the window. With a shattering, splintering sound it passed through, taking most of the frame, the curtain and the curtain rod along with it.

I heard it hit three stories below. When I rose and looked out I saw it twitch a few times and grow still, there on the concrete patio where Julia and I had often had a midnight beer.

I returned to Julia's side and held her hand. I began to realize my anger. Someone had to be behind this. Could it be S again? Was this my April 30 present for this year? I'd a feeling that it was and I wanted to do unto S as I had just done unto the creature that had performed the act. There had to be a reason. There ought to be a clue.

I rose, went to the bedroom, fetched a blanket, and covered Julia with it. Mechanically, I wiped my fingerprints from the fallen doorknob as I began my search of the apartment.

I found them on the mantelpiece between the clock and a stack of paperbacks dealing with the occult. The moment

I touched them and felt their coldness I realized that this was even more serious than I had thought. They had to be the thing of mine she'd had that I would be needing—only they were not really mine, though as I riffled through I recognized them on one level and was puzzled by them on another. They were cards, Trumps, like yet unlike any I had ever seen before.

It was not a complete deck. Just a few cards, actually, and strange. I slipped them into my side pocket quickly when I heard the siren. Time for solitaire later.

I tore down the stairs and out the back door, encountering no one. Fido still lay where he had fallen and all the neighborhood dogs were discussing it. I vaulted fences and trampled flowerbeds, cutting through backyards on my way over to the side street where I was parked.

Minutes later I was miles away, trying to scrub the bloody pawprints from my memory.

CHAPTER 2

I drove away from the bay until I came to a quiet, well-treed area. I stopped the car and got out and walked.

After a long while I located a small, deserted park. I seated myself on one of the benches, took out the Trumps and studied them. A few seemed half familiar and the rest were totally puzzling. I stared too long at one and seemed to hear a siren song. I put them down. I did not recognize the style. This was extremely awkward.

I was reminded of the story of a world-famous toxicologist who inadvertently ingested a poison for which there was no antidote. The question foremost in his mind was, Had he taken a lethal dose? He looked it up in a classic textbook that he himself had written years before. According to his own book he had had it. He checked another, written by an equally eminent professional. According to that one he had taken only about half the amount necessary to do in someone of his body mass. So he sat down and waited, hoping he'd been wrong.

I felt that way because I am an expert on these things. I thought that I knew the work of everyone who might be capable of producing such items. I picked up one of the cards, which held a peculiar, almost familiar fascination for me—depicting a small grassy point jutting out into a quiet lake, a sliver of something bright, glistening, unidentifiable, off to the right. I exhaled heavily upon it, fogging it for an instant, and struck it with my fingernail. It rang like a glass bell and flickered to life. Shadows swam and pulsed as the scene inched into evening. I passed my hand over it and it grew still once again—back to lake, grasses, daytime.

Very distant. Time's stream flowed faster there in relationship to my present situation. Interesting.

I groped for an old pipe with which I sometimes indulge myself, filled it, lit it, puffed it, and mused. The cards were functional all right, not some clever imitations, and though I did not understand their purpose, that was not my main concern at the moment.

Today was April 30, and I had faced death once again. I had yet to confront the person who had been playing with my life. S had again employed a proxy menace. And that was no ordinary dog I had destroyed. And the cards . . . where had Julia gotten them and why had she wanted me to have them? The cards and the dog indicated a power beyond that of an ordinary person. All along I had thought I'd been the subject of the unwelcome attention of some psycho, whom I could deal with at my leisure. But this morning's events put an entirely different complexion on the case. It meant that I had one hell of an enemy somewhere.

I shuddered. I wanted to talk to Luke again, get him to reconstruct their conversation of the previous evening, see whether Julia had said anything that might provide me with a clue. I'd like to go back and search her apartment more carefully, too. But that was out of the question. The cops had pulled up in front of the place as I was driving away. There'd be no getting back in for some time.

Rick. There was Rick Kinsky, the guy she'd begun seeing after we'd broken up. I knew him on sight—a thin, mustached, cerebral sort, thick glasses and all. He managed a bookstore I'd visited once or twice. I didn't know him beyond that, though. Perhaps he could tell me something about the cards and how Julia might have gotten into whatever situation it was that had cost her her life.

I brooded a little longer, then put the cards away. I wasn't about to fool with them any further. Not yet. First, I wanted as much information as I could get.

I headed back for the car. As I walked I reflected that this April 30 wasn't over. Suppose S didn't really consider this morning's encounter as aimed directly at me? In that case there was plenty of time for another attempt. I also had a feeling that if I began getting close S would forget about dates and go for my throat whenever there was an opening. I resolved not to let my guard down at all henceforth, to live as in a state of siege until this matter was settled. And all of my energies were now going to be directed toward settling it. My well-being seemed to require the destruction of my enemy, very soon.

Should I seek counsel? I wondered. And if so, from whom? There was an awful lot I still didn't know about my heritage . . .

No. Not yet, I decided. I had to make every effort to handle things myself. Besides the fact that I wanted to, I needed the practice. It's necessary to be able to deal with nasty matters where I come from.

I drove, looking for a pay phone and trying not to think of Julia as I had last seen her. A few clouds blew in from the west. My watch ticked on my wrist, next to unseen Frakir. The news on the radio was international and cheerless.

I stopped in a drugstore and used a phone there to try to reach Luke at his motel. He wasn't in. So I had a club sandwich and a milkshake in the dining area and tried again afterward. Still out.

Okay. Catch him later. I headed into town. The Browserie, as I recalled, was the name of the bookstore where Rick worked.

I drove by and saw that the place was open. I parked a

couple of blocks up the street and walked back. I had been alert all of the way across town, but could not detect any sign that I was being followed.

A cool breeze touched me as I walked, hinting of rain. I saw Rick through the store's window, seated at his high counter reading a book. There was no one else in sight in the place.

A small bell jangled above the door as I entered, and he looked up. He straightened and his eyes widened as I approached.

"Hi," I said, pausing then for a moment. "Rick, I don't know whether you remember me."

"You're Merle Corey," he stated softly.

"Right." I leaned on the counter and he drew back. "I wondered whether you might be able to help me with a little information."

"What kind of information?"

"It's about Julia," I said.

"Look," he answered, "I never went near her until after you two had broken up."

"Huh? No, no, you don't understand. I don't care about that. It's more recent information that I need. She'd been trying to get in touch with me this past week and—"

He shook his head.

"I haven't heard from her for a couple of months."

"Oh?"

"Yeah, we stopped seeing each other. Different interests, you know?"

"Was she okay when you—stopped seeing each other?"

"I guess so."

I stared straight into his eyes and he winced. I didn't like that. "I guess so." I could see that he was a little afraid of me so I decided to push it.

"What do you mean 'different interests'?" I asked.

"Well, she got a little weird, you know?" he said.

"I don't know. Tell me."

He licked his lips and looked away.

"I don't want any trouble," he stated.

"I'd rather not indulge either. What was the matter?"

"Well," he said, "she was scared."

"Scared? Of what?"

"Uh—of you."

"Me? That's ridiculous. I never did anything to frighten her. What did she say?"

"She never said it in so many words, but I could tell, whenever your name came up. Then she developed all these funny interests."

"You've lost me," I said. "Completely. She got weird? She got funny interests? What kind? What was going on? I really don't understand, and I'd like to."

He got to his feet and headed for the rear of the store, glancing at me as if I should follow him. I did.

He slowed when he reached a section full of books on natural healing and organic farming and martial arts and herbal remedies and having babies at home, but he went on past it into the hardcore occult section.

"Here," he said, halting. "She borrowed a few of these, brought them back, borrowed a few more."

I shrugged.

"That's all? That's hardly weird."

"But she really got into it."

"So do a lot of people."

"Let me finish," he went on. "She started with theosophy, even attended meetings of a local group. She got turned off on it fairly quick, but by then she'd met some people with different connections. Pretty soon she was hanging around with Sufis, Gurdjieffians, even a shaman."

"Interesting," I said. "No yoga?"

"No yoga. When I asked her that same thing she said that it was power she was after, not samadhi. Anyhow, she just kept finding stranger and stranger acquaintances. The atmosphere got too rarefied for me, so I said good-bye."

"I wonder why?" I mused.

"Here," he said, "take a look at this one."

He tossed me a black book and stepped back. I caught

it. It was a copy of the Bible. I opened it to the publishing credits page.

"Something special about this edition?" I asked.

He sighed.

"No. I'm sorry."

He took it back and replaced it on the shelf.

"Just a minute," he said.

He returned to the counter and took a cardboard sign from a shelf beneath it. It read JUST STEPPED OUT. WE'LL REOPEN AT and there was a clock face beneath it with movable hands. He set them to indicate a time a half hour hence and went and hung the sign in the door's window. Then he shot the bolt and gestured for me to follow him to a room in the rear.

The back office contained a desk, a couple of chairs, cartons of books. He seated himself behind the desk and nodded toward the nearest chair. I took it. He switched on a telephone answering machine then, removed a stack of forms and correspondence from the blotter, opened a drawer and took out a bottle of Chianti.

"Care for a glass?" he asked.

"Sure, thanks."

He rose and stepped through the opened door of a small lavatory. He took a pair of glasses from a shelf and rinsed them. He brought them back, set them down, filled both, and pushed one in my direction. They were from the Sheraton.

"Sorry I tossed the Bible at you," he said, raising his glass and taking a sip.

"You looked as if you expected me to go up in a puff of smoke."

He nodded.

"I am really convinced that the reason she wants power has something to do with you. Are you into some form of occultism?"

"No."

"She talked sometimes as if you might even be a supernatural creature yourself."

I laughed. He did, too, after a moment.

"I don't know," he said then. "There're lots of strange things in the world. They can't all be right, but . . ."

I shrugged.

"Who knows? So you think she was looking for some system that would give her power to defend herself against me?"

"That was the impression I got."

I took a drink of the wine.

"That doesn't make sense," I told him.

But even as I said it I knew that it was probably true. And if I had driven her into the path of whatever had destroyed her, then I was partly responsible for her death. I suddenly felt the burden along with the pain.

"Finish the story," I said.

"That's pretty much it," he answered. "I got tired of people who wanted to discuss cosmic crap all the time and I split."

"And that's all? Did she find the right system, the right guru? What happened?"

He took a big drink and stared at me.

"I really liked her," he said.

"I'm sure."

"The Tarot, Caballa, Golden Dawn, Crowley, Fortune—that's where she went next."

"Did she stay?"

"I don't know for sure. But I think so. I only heard this after a while."

"Ritual magic, then?"

"Probably."

"Who does it?"

"Lots of people."

"I mean who did she find? Did you hear that?"

"I think it was Victor Melman."

He looked at me expectantly. I shook my head.

"I'm sorry. I don't know the name."

"Strange man," he mused, taking a sip and leaning back in his chair, clasping his hands behind his neck and bringing

his elbows forward. He stared off into the lavatory. "I—
I've heard it said—by a number of people, some of them
fairly reliable—that he really has something going for him,
that he has a hold on a piece of something, that he's known
a kind of enlightenment, has been initiated, has a sort of
power and is sometimes a great teacher. But he's got these
ego problems, too, that seem to go along with that sort of
thing. And there's a touch of the seamy side there. I've
even heard it said that that's not his real name, that he's got
a record, and there's more of Manson to him than Magus.
I don't know. He's nominally a painter—actually a pretty
good one. His stuff does sell."

"You've met him?"

A pause, then, "Yes."

"What were your own impressions?"

"I don't know. Well . . . I'm prejudiced. I can't really
say."

I swirled the wine in my glass.

"How come?"

"Oh, I wanted to study with him once. He turned me
down."

"So you were into this, too. I thought—"

"I'm not into anything," he snapped. "I tried everything
at some time or other, I mean. Everybody goes through
phases. I wanted to develop, expand, advance. Who doesn't?
But I never found it." He unbent and took another gulp of
wine. "Sometimes I felt that I was close, that there was
some power, some vision that I could almost touch or see.
Almost. Then it was gone. It's all a lot of crap. You just
delude yourself. Sometimes I even thought I had it. Then
a few days would go by and I realized that I was lying to
myself again."

"All of this was before you met Julia?"

He nodded.

"Right. That might be what held us together for a while.
I still like to talk about all this bullshit, even if I don't
believe it anymore. Then she got too serious about it, and
I didn't feel like going that route again."

"I see."

He drained his glass and refilled it.

"There's nothing to any of it," he said. "There are an infinite number of ways of lying to yourself, of rationalizing things into something they are not. I guess that I wanted magic, and there is no real magic in the world."

"That why you threw the Bible at me?"

He snorted.

"It could as easily have been the Koran or the Vedas, I suppose. It would have been neat to see you vanish in a flash of fire. But no go."

I smiled.

"How can I find Melman?"

"I've got it here somewhere," he said, lowering his eyes and opening a drawer. "Here."

He withdrew a small notebook and flipped through it. He copied out an address on an index card and handed it to me. He took another drink of wine.

"Thanks."

"It's his studio, but he lives there, too," he added.

I nodded and set down my glass.

"I appreciate everything you told me."

He raised the bottle.

"Have another drink?"

"No, thanks."

He shrugged and topped off his own. I rose.

"You know, it's really sad," he said.

"What?"

"That there's no magic, that there never was, there probably never will be."

"That's the breaks," I said.

"The world would be a lot more interesting place."

"Yeah."

I turned to go.

"Do me a favor," he said.

"What?"

"On the way out, set that sign for three o'clock and let the bolt in the door snap shut again."

"Sure."

I left him there and did those things. The sky had grown a lot darker, the wind a bit more chill. I tried again to reach Luke, from a phone on the corner, but he was still out.

We were happy. It had been a terrific day. The weather was perfect, and everything we did had worked out right. We went to a fun party that evening and afterward had a late dinner at a really good little place we'd stumbled upon by accident. We lingered over drinks, hating for the day to end. We decided then to prolong a winning streak, and we drove to an otherwise deserted beach where we sat around and splashed around and watched the moon and felt the breezes. For a long while. I did something then that I had sort of promised myself I would not. Hadn't Faust thought a beautiful moment worth a soul?

"Come on," I said, aiming my beer can at a trash bin and catching hold of her hand. "Let's take a walk."

"Where to?" she asked, as I drew her to her feet.

"Fairy land," I replied. "The fabled realms of yore. Eden. Come on."

Laughing, she let me lead her along the beach, toward a place where it narrowed, squeezing by high embankments. The moon was generous and yellow, the sea sang my favorite song.

We strolled hand in hand past the bluffs, where a quick turning of the way took us out of sight of our stretch of sand. I looked for the cave that should be occurring soon, high and narrow . . .

"A cave," I announced moments later. "Let's go in."

"It'll be dark."

"Good," I said, and we entered.

The moonlight followed us for about six paces. By then, though, I had spotted the turnoff to the left.

"This way," I stated.

"It *is* dark!"

"Sure. Just keep hold of me a little longer. It'll be okay."

Fifteen or twenty steps and there was a faint illumination

to the right. I led her along that turning and the way brightened as we advanced.

"We may get lost," she said softly.

"I don't get lost," I answered her.

It continued to brighten. The way turned once more, and we proceeded along that last passage to emerge at the foot of a mountain in sight of a low forest, the sun standing at midmorning height above its trees.

She froze, blue eyes wide.

"It's daytime!" she said.

"Tempus fugit," I replied. "Come on."

We walked through the woods for a time, listening to the birds and the breezes, dark-haired Julia and I, and I led her after a while through a canyon of colored rocks and grasses, beside a stream that flowed into a river.

We followed the river until we came, abruptly, to a precipice from whence it plunged a mighty distance, casting rainbows and fogs. Standing there, staring out across the great valley that lay below, we beheld a city of spires and cupolas, gilt and crystal, through morning and mist.

"Where—are we?" she asked.

"Just around the corner," I said. "Come."

I led her to the left, then down a trail that took us back along the face of the cliff, passing finally behind the cataract. Shadows and diamond beads . . . a roaring to approach the power of silence . . .

We passed at last into a tunnel, damp at first but drying as it rose. We followed it to a gallery, open to our left and looking out upon night and stars, stars, stars. . . . It was an enormous prospect, blazing with new constellations, their light sufficient to cast our shadows onto the wall behind us. She leaned over the low parapet, her skin some rare polished marble, and she looked downward.

"They're down there, too," she said. "And to both sides! There is nothing below but more stars. And to the sides . . ."

"Yes. Pretty things, aren't they?"

We remained there for a long while, watching, before I could persuade her to come away and follow the tunnel farther. It bore us out again to behold a ruined classical amphitheater beneath a late afternoon sky. Ivy grew over broken benches and fractured pillars. Here and there lay a shattered statue, as if cast down by earthquake. Very picturesque. I'd thought she'd like it, and I was right. We took turns seating ourselves and speaking to each other. The acoustics were excellent.

We walked away then, hand in hand, down myriad ways beneath skies of many colors, coming at last in sight of a quiet lake with a sun entering evening upon its farther shore. There was a glittering mass of rock off to my right. We walked out upon a small point cushioned with mosses and ferns.

I put my arms around her and we stood there for a long time, and the wind in the trees was lute song counterpointed by invisible birds. Later still, I unbuttoned her blouse.

"Right here?" she said.

"I like it here. Don't you?"

"It's beautiful. Okay. Wait a minute."

So we lay down and loved till the shadows covered us. After a time she slept, as I desired.

I set a spell upon her to keep her asleep, for I was beginning to have second thoughts over the wisdom of making this journey. Then I dressed both of us and picked her up to carry her back. I took a shortcut.

On the beach from which we'd started I put her down and stretched out beside her. Soon I slept also.

We did not awaken till after the sun was up, when the sounds of bathers roused us.

She sat up and stared at me.

"Last night," she said, "could not have been a dream. But it couldn't have been real either. Could it?"

"I guess so," I said.

She furrowed her brow.

"What did you just agree to?" she asked.

"Breakfast," I said. "Let's go get some. Come on."

"Wait a minute." She put a hand on my arm. "Something unusual happened. What was it?"

"Why destroy the magic by talking about it? Let's go eat."

She questioned me a lot in the days that followed, but I was adamant in refusing to talk about it. Stupid, the whole thing was stupid. I should never have taken her on that walk. It contributed to that final argument that set us permanently apart.

And now, driving, as I thought about it, I realized something more than my stupidity. I realized that I had been in love with her, that I still loved her. Had I not taken her on that walk, or had I acknowledged her later accusation that I was a sorcerer, she would not have taken the route that she took, seeking power of her own—probably for self-protection. She would be alive.

I bit my lip and cried out. I cut around the braking car in front of me and crashed a light. If I had killed the thing I loved, I was certain that the opposite was not going to be true.

CHAPTER 3

Grief and anger shrink my world, and I resent this. They seem to paralyze my memory of happier times, of friends, places, things, options. Squeezed by the grip of intense, unsettling emotion, I grow smaller in my single-mindedness. I suppose it is partly because I have discarded a range of choices, impairing in some measure my freedom of will. I don't like this, but after a point I have small control over it. It makes me feel that I have surrendered to a kind of determinism, which irritates me even more. Then, vicious cycle, this feeds back into the emotion that drives me and intensifies it. The simple way of ending this situation is the headlong rush to remove its object. The difficult way is more philosophical, a drawing back, the reestablishment of control. As usual, the difficult way is preferable. A headlong rush may also result in a broken neck.

I parked in the first place that I saw, opened the window, lit my pipe. I vowed not to depart until I had grown calm. All of my life I have had a tendency to overreact to things. It seems to run in my family. But I did not want to be like the others. They made a lot of trouble for themselves that way. The full-scale, all-or-nothing reaction may be all right if you always win, but that way also lies high tragedy or at least opera if you happen to be up against something extraordinary. And I did have indications that this was the case. Therefore, I was a fool. I told myself this till I believed it.

Then I listened to my calmer self as it agreed that I was indeed a fool—for not having seen my own feelings when I could have done something about them, for having displayed a power and denied its consequences, for not having at least guessed at the strange nature of my enemy in all these years, for my present simplification of the coming encounter. It would not do to seize Victor Melman on sight and try to beat the truth out of him. I resolved to proceed carefully, covering myself at all times. Life is never simple, I told myself. Sit still and gather, regroup.

Slowly, I felt the tension go out of me. Slowly, too, my world grew again, and I saw within it the possibility that S really knew me, knew me well, and may even have arranged events so that I would dispense with thinking and surrender to the moment. No, I would not be like the others...

I sat there and thought for a long while before I started the engine again and drove on slowly.

It was a grimy brick building situated on a corner. It was four stories in height, with occasional spray-painted obscenities on the alley side and on the wall facing the narrower street. I discovered the graffiti, a few broken windows and the fire escape as I strolled slowly about the place, looking it over. By then a light rain was just beginning to fall. The lower two stories were occupied by the Brutus Storage Company, according to a sign beside the stairs in a small hallway I entered. The place smelled of urine, and there was an empty Jack Daniels bottle lying on the dusty windowsill to my right. Two mailboxes hung upon the flaking wall. One said "Brutus Storage," the other bore the legend "V.M." Both were empty.

I mounted the stair, expecting it to creak. It did not. There were four knobless doors letting upon the second-floor hallway, all of them closed. The outlines of what might be cartons were visible through several of the frosted panes in their upper sections. There were no sounds from within.

I surprised a black cat dozing on the next stairway. She arched her back, showed me her teeth, made a hissing noise, then turned and bounded up the stairs and out of sight.

The next landing also had four doors—three of them apparently nonfunctional, the fourth dark-stained and shellacked shiny. It bore a small brass plate that read "Melman." I knocked.

There was no answer. I tried again several times, with the same result. No sounds from within either. It seemed likely that these were his living quarters and that the fourth floor, with the possibility of a skylight, held his studio. So I turned away and took the final flight.

I reached the top and saw that one of the four doors there was slightly ajar. I halted and listened for a moment. From beyond it came faint sounds of movement. I advanced and gave it a few knocks. I heard a sudden intake of breath from somewhere inside. I pushed on the door.

He stood about twenty feet away beneath a large skylight and he had turned to face me—a tall, broad-shouldered man with dark beard and eyes. He held a brush in his left hand and a palette in his right. He wore a paint-smeared apron over his Levi's and had on a plaid sport shirt. The easel at his back held the outlines of what could be a madonna and child. There were a great many other canvases about, all of them facing the walls or covered.

"Hello," I said. "You are Victor Melman?"

He nodded, neither smiling nor frowning, placed his palette on a nearby table, his brush into a jar of solvent. He picked up a damp-looking cloth then and wiped his hands with it.

"And yourself?" he asked, tossing the cloth aside and facing me again.

"Merle Corey. You knew Julia Barnes."

"I don't deny it," he said. "Your use of the past tense would seem to indicate—"

"She's dead all right. I want to talk to you about it."

"All right," he said, untying his apron. "Let's go downstairs then. No place to sit up here."

He hung the apron upon a nail near the door and stepped outside. I followed him. He turned back and locked the studio before proceeding down the stairs. His movements were smooth, almost graceful. I could hear the rain on the roof.

He used the same key to unlock the dark door on the third floor. He drew the door open and stood aside, gesturing for me to enter. I did, traversing a hallway that led past a kitchen, its counters covered with empty bottles, stacks of dishes, pizza cartons. Bursting bags of trash leaned against cupboards; the floor looked sticky here and there and the place smelled like a spice factory next door to a slaughterhouse.

The living room, which I came to next, was large, with a comfortable-looking pair of black sofas, facing each other across a battlefield of Oriental carpets and miscellaneous tables, each of which bore several overflowing ashtrays. There was a beautiful concert-sized piano in the far corner, before a wall covered with heavy red drapery. There were numerous low bookcases filled with occult materials, stacks of magazines beside them, atop them, and alongside a few easy chairs. What could be the corner of a pentacle protruded slightly from beneath the largest rug. The stale smells of incense and pot lingered in patches. To my right, there was an archway leading to another room, a closed door to my left. Paintings of a semireligious nature—which I took to be his work—were hung on several of the walls. There was a Chagall-like quality to them. Quite good.

"Have a seat."

He gestured toward an easy chair and I took it.

"Care for a beer?"

"Thank you, no."

He seated himself on the nearer sofa, clasped his hands, and stared at me.

"What happened?" he asked.

I stared back at him.

"Julia Barnes got interested in occult systems," I said. "She came to you to learn more about them. She died this morning under very unusual circumstances."

The left corner of his mouth twitched slightly. He made no other movement.

"Yes, she was interested in such matters," he said. "She came to me for instruction and I provided it."

"I want to know why she died."

He continued to stare.

"Her time was up," he said. "It happens to everybody, in the long run."

"She was killed by an animal that should not exist here. Do you know anything about it?"

"The universe is a stranger place than most of us can imagine."

"Do you know or don't you?"

"I know you," he said, smiling for the first time. "She spoke of you, of course."

"What does that mean?"

"It means," he answered, "that I know you are more than a little aware of such matters yourself."

"And so?"

"The Arts have a way of bringing the right people together at the proper moment when there is work in progress."

"And that's what you think this is all about?"

"I know it."

"How?"

"It was promised."

"So you were expecting me?"

"Yes."

"Interesting. Would you care to tell me more about it?"

"I'd rather show you."

"You say that something was promised. How? By whom?"

"All of that will become clear shortly."

"And Julia's death?"

"That, too, I'd say."

"How do you propose rendering me this enlightenment?"

He smiled. "I just want you to take a look at something," he said.

"All right. I'm willing. Show me."

He nodded and rose.

"It's in here," he explained, turning and heading toward the closed door.

I got to my feet and followed him across the room.

He reached into his shirtfront and drew up a chain. He lifted it over his head and I could see that it bore a key. He used it to unlock the door.

"Go in," he said, pushing it open and stepping aside.

I entered. It was not a large room, and it was dark. He flipped a switch and a blue light of small wattage came on within a plain fixture overhead. I saw then that there was one window, directly across from me, and that all of its panes had been painted black. There were no furnishings save for a few cushions scattered here and there across the floor. A portion of the wall to my right was covered with black drapery. The other walls were unadorned.

"I'm looking," I said.

He chuckled.

"A moment, a moment," he advised me. "Have you any idea of my major concern in the occult arts?"

"You're a cabalist," I stated.

"Yes," he admitted. "How could you tell?"

"People in Eastern disciplines tend to run a tight ship," I stated. "But cabalists always seem to be slobs."

He snorted.

"It is all a matter of what is really important to you," he said then.

"Exactly."

He kicked a cushion into the middle of the floor.

"Have a seat," he said.

"I'll stand."

He shrugged.

"Okay," he said, and he began muttering softly.

I waited. After a time, still speaking quietly, he moved

to the black curtain. He opened it with a single quick movement and I stared.

A painting of the cabalistic Tree of Life was revealed, showing the ten sephira in some of their qlipphotic aspects. It was beautifully executed, and the sense of recognition that struck me as I regarded it was unsettling. It was no standard item from some head shop, but rather an original painting. It was not, however, in the style of any of the works hanging in the other room. Still, it was familiar to me.

As I studied it I had no doubt whatsoever that it had been painted by the same person who had done the Trumps I had found in Julia's apartment.

Melman continued his incantation as I regarded the painting.

"Is this your work?" I asked him.

He did not answer me. Instead, he advanced and pointed, indicating the third sephiroth, the one called Binah. I studied it. It seemed to represent a wizard before a dark altar, and—

No! I couldn't believe it. It shouldn't—

I felt a contact with that figure. It was not just symbolic. He was real, and he was summoning me. He loomed larger, grew three-dimensional. The room began to fade about me. I was almost—

There.

It was a place of twilight, a small glade in a twisted wood. An almost bloody light illuminated the slab before me. The wizard, his face hidden by cowl and shadow, manipulated objects upon the stone, his hands moving too rapidly for me to follow. From somewhere, I still seemed to hear the chanting, faintly.

Finally, he raised a single object in his right hand and held it steady. It was a black, obsidian dagger. He laid his left arm upon the altar and brushed it across the surface, sweeping everything else to the ground.

He looked at me for the first time.

"Come here," he said then.

I began to smile at the stupid simplicity of the request.

But then I felt my feet move without my willing them to do so, and I knew that a spell lay upon me in this dark shadow.

I thanked another uncle, who dwelled in the most distant place imaginable, as I began to speak in Thari, a spell of my own.

A piercing cry, as of some swooping night bird, rent the air.

The wizard was not distracted, nor my feet freed, but I was able to raise my arms before me. I kept them at the proper level, and when they reached the forward edge of the altar I cooperated with the summoning spell, increasing the force of each automatonlike step that I took. I let my elbows bend.

The wizard was already swinging the blade toward my fingers, but it didn't matter. I put all of my weight behind it and heaved at the stone.

The altar toppled backward. The wizard scurried to avoid it, but it struck one—perhaps both—of his legs. Immediately, as he fell to the ground, I felt the spell depart from me. I could move properly again and my mind was clear.

He drew his knees up to his chest and began to roll even as I leaped over the wrecked altar and reached toward him. I moved to follow as he somersaulted down a small slope and passed between two standing stones and into the darkened wood.

As soon as I reached the clearing's edge I saw eyes, hundreds of feral eyes blazing from the darkness at many levels. The incanting grew louder, seemed nearer, seemed to be coming from behind me.

I turned quickly.

The altar was still in wreckage. Another cowled figure stood behind it, much larger than the first. This one was doing the chanting, in a familiar masculine voice. Frakir pulsed upon my wrist. I felt a spell building about me, but this time I was not unprepared. The opposite of my walk, a summons, brought an icy wind that swept the spell away like so much smoke. My garments were lashed about me,

changing shape and color. Purple, gray . . . light the trousers
and dark the cloak, the shirtfront. Black my boots and wide
belt, my gauntlets tucked behind, my silver Frakir woven
into a bracelet about my left wrist, visible now and shining.
I raised my left hand and shielded my eyes with my right,
as I summoned a flash of light.

"Be silent," I said then. "You offend me."

The chanting ceased.

The cowl was blown back from his head and I regarded
Melman's frightened face.

"All right. You wanted me," I stated, "and now you have
me, heaven help you. You said that everything would become
clear to me. It hasn't. Make it clear."

I took a step forward.

"Talk!" I said. "It can be easy or it can be hard. But you
will talk. The choice is yours."

He threw back his head and bellowed: "Master!"

"Summon your master then, by any means," I said. "I
will wait. For he, too, must answer."

He called out again, but there was no answer. He bolted
then, but I was ready for this with a major summoning. The
woods decayed and fell before he could reach them, and
then they moved, were swept up in a mighty wind where
there should be stillness. It circled the glade, gray and red,
building an impenetrable wall to infinites above and below.
We inhabited a circular island in the night, several hundred
meters across, its edges slowly crumbling.

"He is not coming," I said, "and you are not going. He
cannot help you. No one will help you. This is a place of
high magic and you profane it with your presence. Do you
know what lies beyond the advancing winds? Chaos. I will
give you to it now, unless you tell me about Julia and your
master and why you dared to bring me here."

He drew back from the Chaos and turned to face me.

"Take me back to my apartment and I will tell you everything," he said.

I shook my head.

"Kill me and you will never know."

I shrugged.

"In that case, you will tell me in order to stop the pain. Then I will give you to the Chaos."

I moved toward him.

"Wait!" He raised his hand. "Give me my life for what I am about to tell you."

"No bargain. Talk."

The winds swirled around us and our island shrank. Half-heard, half-intelligible voices babbled within the wind and fragments of forms swam there. Melman drew back from the crumbling edge of things.

"All right," he said, speaking loudly. "Yes, Julia came to me, as I had been told she would, and I taught her some things—not the things I would have taught her even a year ago, but pieces of some new things I had only learned myself more recently. I had been told to teach her in this manner, also."

"By whom? Name your master."

He grimaced.

"He was not so foolish as to give me his name," he said, "that I might seek some control over him. Like yourself, he is not human, but a being from some other plane."

"He gave you the painting of the Tree?"

Melman nodded.

"Yes, and it actually transported me to each sephiroth. Magic worked in those places. I gained powers."

"And the Trumps? He did those, too? He gave them to you to give to her?"

"I don't know anything about any Trumps," he answered.

"These!" I cried, drawing them from beneath my cloak, spreading them like a conjurer's fan and advancing toward him. I thrust them at him and let him stare for a few moments, withdrawing them before he got the idea that they might represent a means of escape.

"I never saw them before," he said.

The ground continued its steady erosion toward us. We withdrew to a point nearer the center.

"And you sent the creature that slew her?"

He shook his head vehemently.

"I did not. I knew that she was going to die, for he had told me that that was what would bring you to me. He told me, too, that it would be a beast from Netzach that would slay her—but I never saw it and I had no part in its summoning."

"And why did he want you to meet me, to bring me here?"

He laughed wildly.

"Why?" he repeated. "To kill you, of course. He told me that if I could sacrifice you in this place I would gain your powers. He said that you are Merlin, son of Hell and Chaos, and that I would become the greatest mage of all could I slay you here."

Our world was at best a hundred meters across now, and the rate of its shrinkage was accelerating.

"Was it true?" he asked. "Would I have gained had I succeeded?"

"Power is like money," I said. "You can usually get it if you're competent and it's the only thing you want in life. Would you have gained by it, though? I don't think so."

"I'm talking about the meaning of life. You know that."

I shook my head.

"Only a fool believes that life has but one meaning," I said. "Enough of this! Describe your master."

"I never saw him."

"What?"

"I mean, I saw him but I don't know what he looks like. He always wore a hood and a black trench coat. Gloves, too. I don't even know his race."

"How did you meet?"

"He appeared one day in my studio. I just turned around and he was standing there. He offered me power, said that he would teach me things in return for my service."

"How did you know he could deliver?"

"He took me on a journey through places not of this world."

"I see."

Our island of existence was now about the size of a large living room. The voices of the wind were mocking, then compassionate, frightened, sad and angry, too. Our wrap-around vision shifted constantly. The ground trembled without letup. The light was still baleful. A part of me wanted to kill Melman right then, but if he had not really been the one who had hurt Julia . . .

"Did your master tell you why he wanted me dead?" I asked him.

He licked his lips and glanced back at the advancing Chaos.

"He said that you were his enemy," he explained, "but he never told me why. And he said that it was going to happen today, that he wanted it to happen today."

"Why today?"

He smiled briefly.

"I suppose because it's Walpurgisnacht," he replied, "though he never actually said that."

"That's all?" I said. "He never mentioned where he was from?"

"He once referred to something called the Keep of the Four Worlds as if it were important to him."

"And you never felt that he was simply using you?"

He smiled. "Of course he was using me," he replied. "We all use somebody. That is the way of the world. But he paid for this use with knowledge and power. And I think his promise may yet be fulfilled."

He seemed to be glancing at something behind me. It was the oldest trick in the world, but I turned. There was no one there. Immediately, I spun back to face him.

He held the black dagger. It must have been up his sleeve. He lunged at me, thrusting, mouthing fresh incantations.

I stepped back and swirled my cloak at him. He disengaged himself, sidestepping and slashing, turned and advanced again. This time he came in low, trying to circle me, his lips still moving. I kicked at the knifehand, but he snapped it back. I caught up the left edge of my cloak then, wrapped it about my arm. When he struck again, I blocked the thrust and seized his biceps. Dropping lower as I drew him forward, I caught hold of his left thigh with my right hand, then straightened, raising him high in the air, and threw him.

As I turned my body, completing the throw, I realized what I had done. Too late. With my attention focused on my adversary I had not kept track of the rapid, grinding advance of the destroying winds. The edge of Chaos was much nearer than I had thought, and Melman had time for only the most abbreviated of curses before death took him where he would incant no more.

I cursed, too, because I was certain there was still more information that I could have gotten from him; and I shook my head, there at the center of my diminishing world.

The day was not yet over and it was already my most memorable Walpurgisnacht ever.

CHAPTER 4

It was a long walk back. I changed my clothes on the way.

My exit from the labyrinth took the form of a narrow alleyway between a pair of dirty brick buildings. It was still raining and the day had made its way into evening. I saw my parked car across the street at the edge of a pool of light cast by one of the unbroken streetlamps. I thought wistfully for a moment of my dry garments in the trunk, then I headed back toward the Brutus Storage sign.

A small light burned within the first-floor office, spilling a little illumination into the otherwise dark entranceway. I trudged on up the stairs, terminally moist and reasonably alert. The apartment door opened when I turned the knob and pushed. I switched on the light and entered, bolting the door behind me.

A quick prowl showed me that the place was deserted, and I changed out of my wet shirt into one from Melman's closet. His trousers were too big in the waist and a bit long for me, though. I transferred my Trumps to a breast pocket to keep them dry.

Step two. I began a systematic ransacking of the place.

After a few minutes, I came across his occult diary in a locked drawer in his bedside table. It was as messy as the rest of the place, with misspellings, crossed-out words, and a few beer and coffee stains. It seemed to contain a lot of derivative stuff mixed with the usual subjective business— dreams and meditations. I flipped farther along in it, looking for the place where he'd met his master. I came to it and skimmed along. It was lengthy, and seemed mostly comprised of enthusiastic ejaculations over the workings of the Tree he had been given. I decided to save it for later and was about to stow it when a final riffling of the pages brought a brief poem into view. Swinburnian, overly allusive and full of rapture, the lines that first caught my eye were, "—the infinite shadows of Amber, touched with her treacherous taint." Too much alliteration, but it was the thought that counted. It revived my earlier feeling of vulnerability and caused me to ransack faster. I suddenly wanted only to get out, get far away and think.

The room held no further surprises. I departed it, gathered an armload of strewn newspapers, carried them to the john, tossed them into the bathtub, and set fire to them, opening the window on the way out. I visited the sanctum then, fetched out the Tree of Life painting, brought it back and added it to the blaze. I switched off the bathroom light and closed the door as I left. I'm one hell of an art critic.

I headed for the stacks of miscellaneous papers on the bookshelves then and began a disappointing search among them. I was halfway through my second heap when the telephone rang.

The world seemed to freeze as my thoughts sprinted. Of course. Today was the day when I was supposed to find my way here and be killed. Chances seemed decent that if it were going to happen it would have happened by now. So this could well be S, calling to learn whether my obituary had been posted. I turned and located the phone, back on the shadowy wall near the bedroom. I had known immediately that I was going to answer it. Moving toward it, I was allowing two to three rings—twelve to eighteen seconds—in which to decide whether my response was to consist of a wisecrack, an insult and a threat, or whether I was going to try to fake it and see what I might learn. As satisfying as the former could be, spoilsport prudence dictated the latter course and also suggested I confine myself to low monosyllables and pretend to be injured and out of breath. I raised the receiver, ready to hear S's voice at last and find out whether I knew him.

"Yes?" I said.

"Well? Is it done?" came the response.

Damn pronoun. It was a woman. Wrong gender but a rightsounding question. One out of two isn't bad, though.

I exhaled heavily, then: "Yeah."

"What's the matter?"

"I'm hurt," I croaked.

"Is it serious?"

"Think so. Got something—here—though. Better come—see."

"What is it? Something of his?"

"Yeah. Can't talk. Getting dizzy. Come."

I cradled the phone and smiled. I thought it very well played. I'd a feeling I'd taken her in completely.

I crossed the living room to the same chair I had occupied earlier, drew up one of the small tables bearing a large ashtray, seated myself, and reached for my pipe. Time to rest, cultivate patience, think a bit.

Moments later I felt a familiar, almost electrical tingling. I was on my feet in an instant, snatching up the ashtray, butts flying like bullets about me, cursing my stupidity yet again as I looked frantically about the room.

There! Before the red drapes, beside the piano. Taking form...

I waited for the full outline, then hurled the ashtray as hard as I could.

An instant later she was there—tall, russet-haired, dark-eyed, holding what looked like a .38 automatic.

The ashtray hit her in the stomach and she doubled forward with a gasp.

I was there before she could straighten.

I jerked the gun out of her hand and threw it across the room. Then I seized both her wrists, spun her around and seated her hard in the nearest chair. In her left hand she still held a Trump. I snatched it away. It was a representation of this apartment, and it was done in the same style as the Tree and the cards in my pocket.

"Who are you?" I snarled.

"Jasra," she spat back, "dead man!"

She opened her mouth wide and her head fell forward. I felt the moist touch of her lips upon the back of my left forearm, which still held her own right wrist against the chair's arm. Seconds later I felt an excruciating pain there. It was not a bite, but rather felt as if a fiery nail had been driven into my flesh.

I let go her wrist and jerked my arm away. The movement was strangely slow, weakened. A cold, tingling sensation moved down into the hand and up along the arm. My hand dropped to my side and seemed to go away. She extricated herself easily from my grip, smiled, placed her fingertips lightly upon my chest and pushed.

I fell backward. I was ridiculously weak and I couldn't control my movements. I felt no pain when I struck the floor, and it was a real effort to turn my head to regard her as she rose to her feet.

"Enjoy it," she stated. "After you awaken, the remainder of your brief existence will be painful."

She passed out of my line of sight, and moments later I heard her raise the telephone receiver.

I was certain she was phoning S, and I believed what she had just said. At least, I would get to meet the mysterious artist . . .

Artist! I twitched the fingers of my right hand. They still functioned, albeit slowly. Straining every bit of will and anatomy that remained under my control, I tried then to raise the hand to my chest. The movement that followed was a jerky, slow-motion thing. At least I had fallen upon my left side, and my back masked this feeble activity from the woman who had done me in.

My hand was trembling and seemed to be slowing even more when it came to the breast pocket. For ages after, I seemed to pick at the edges of pieces of pasteboard. Finally, one came free and I was able to twitch it high enough to view it. By then I was very dizzy and my vision was beginning to blur. I wasn't certain I could manage the transfer. From across a vast distance I could hear Jasra's voice as she conversed with someone, but I was unable to distinguish the words.

I focused what remained of my attention upon the card. It was a sphinx, crouched upon a blue, rocky ledge. I reached for it. Nothing. My mind felt as if it were embedded in cotton. I possessed barely enough consciousness for one more attempt.

I felt a certain coldness and seemed to see the sphinx move slightly upon its stony shelf. I felt as if I were falling forward into a black wave that was rushing upward.

And that was all.

I was a long time coming around. My consciousness dribbled back, but my limbs were still leaden and my vision clouded. The lady's sting seemed to have delivered a neurotropic toxin. I tried flexing my fingers and toes and could not be certain whether I'd succeeded. I tried to speed up and deepen my breathing. That worked, anyway.

After a time, I heard what seemed a roaring sound. It stepped itself down a little later, and I realized it was my own rushing blood in my ears. A while after that I felt my heartbeat, and my vision began to clear. Light and dark and shapelessness resolved into sand and rocks. I felt little areas of chill, all over. Then I began to shiver, and this passed and I realized that I could move. But I felt very weak, so I didn't. Not for a while.

I heard noises—rustlings, stirrings—coming from somewhere above and before me. I also became aware of a peculiar odor.

"I say, are you awake?" This from the same direction as the sounds of movement.

I decided that I was not entirely ready to qualify for that state, so I did not answer. I waited for more life to flow back into my limbs.

"I really wish you'd let me know whether you can hear me," the voice came again. "I'd like to get on with it."

My curiosity finally overcame my judgment and I raised my head.

"There! I knew it!"

On the blue-gray ledge above me was crouched a sphinx, also blue—lion body, large feathered wings folded tight against it, a genderless face looking down upon me. It licked its lips and revealed a formidable set of teeth.

"Get on with what?" I asked, raising myself slowly into a sitting position and drawing several deep breaths.

"The riddling," it answered, "the thing I do best."

"I'll take a rain check," I said, waiting for the cramps in my arms and legs to pass.

"Sorry. I must insist."

I rubbed my punctured forearm and glared at the creature. Most of the stories I recalled about sphinxes involved their devouring people who couldn't answer riddles. I shook my head.

"I won't play your game," I said.

"In that case, you lose by forfeit," it replied, shoulder muscles beginning to tighten.

"Hold on," I said, raising my hand. "Give me a minute or two to recover and I'll probably feel differently."

It settled back and said, "Okay. That would make it more official. Take five. Let me know when you're ready."

I climbed to my feet and began swinging my arms and stretching. While I was about it, I surveyed the area quickly.

We occupied a sandy arroyo, punctuated here and there with orange, gray, and blue rocks. The stony wall whose ledge the sphinx occupied rose steeply before me to a height of perhaps twenty-five feet; another wall of the same height lay at about that distance to my rear. The wash rose steeply to my right, ran off in a more level fashion to my left. A few spiky green shrubs inhabited rifts and crevices. The hour seemed verging upon dusk. The sky was a weak yellow with no sun in sight. I heard a distant wind but did not feel it. The place was cool but not chill.

I spotted a rock the size of a small dumbbell on the ground nearby. Two ambling paces—as I continued swinging my arms and stretching—and it lay beside my right foot.

The sphinx cleared its throat.

"Are you ready?" it asked.

"No," I said. "But I'm sure that won't stop you."

"You're right."

I felt an uncontrollable desire to yawn and did so.

"You seem to lack something of the proper spirit," it observed. "But here it is: I rise in flame from the earth. The wind assails me and waters lash me. Soon I will oversee all things."

I waited. Perhaps a minute passed.

"Well?" the sphinx finally said.

"Well what?"

"Have you the answer?"

"To what?"

"The riddle, of course!"

"I was waiting. There was no question, only a series of statements. I can't answer a question if I don't know what it is."

"It's a time-honored format. The interrogative is implied by the context. Obviously, the question is, 'What am I?'"

"It could just as easily be, 'Who is buried in Grant's tomb?' But okay. What is it? The phoenix, of course—nested upon the earth, rising in flames above it, passing through the air, the clouds, to a great height—"

"Wrong."

It smiled and began to stir.

"Hold on," I said. "It is not wrong. It fits. It may not be the answer you want, but it is an answer that meets the requirements."

It shook its head.

"I am the final authority on these answers. I do the defining."

"Then you cheat."

"I do not!"

"I drink off half the contents of a flask. Does that make it half full or half empty?"

"Either. Both."

"Exactly. Same thing. If more than one answer fits, you have to buy them all. It's like waves and particles."

"I don't like that approach," it stated. "It would open all sorts of doors to ambiguity. It could spoil the riddling business."

"Not my fault," I said, clenching and unclenching my hands.

"But you do raise an interesting point."

I nodded vigorously.

"But there *should* only be one correct answer."

I shrugged.

"We inhabit a less than ideal world," I suggested.

"Hm."

"We could just call it a tie," I offered. "Nobody wins, nobody loses."

"I find that esthetically displeasing."

"It works okay in lots of other games."

"Also, I've grown a bit hungry."

"The truth surfaces."

"But I am not unfair. I serve the truth, in my fashion. Your mention of a tie raises the possibility of a solution."

"Good. I'm glad you see things—"

"That being a tie breaker. Ask me your riddle."

"This is silly," I said. "I don't have any riddles."

"Then you'd better come up with one fast. Because it's the only way out of our deadlock—that, or I judge you the loser."

I swung my arms and did a few deep kneebends. My body felt as if it were afire. It also felt stronger.

"Okay," I said. "Okay. Just a second."

What the hell . . .

"What's green and red and goes round and round and round?"

The sphinx blinked twice, then furrowed its brow. I used the time that followed for some more deep breathing and some running in place. The fires subsided, my head grew clearer, my pulse steadied . . .

"Well?" I said some minutes later.

"I'm thinking."

"Take your time."

I did a little shadowboxing. Did some isometrics, too. The sky had darkened a bit more and a few stars were now visible off to my right.

"Uh, I hate to rush you," I said, "but—"

The sphinx snorted. "I'm still thinking."

"Maybe we should set a time limit."

"It shouldn't be much longer."

"Mind if I rest?"

"Go ahead."

I stretched out on the sand and closed my eyes, muttering a guard word to Frakir before I slept.

I woke with a shiver, light in my eyes and a breeze upon my face. It took me several moments to realize that it was morning. The sky was brightening to my left, stars were fading to my right. I was thirsty. Hungry, too.

I rubbed my eyes. I got to my feet. I located my comb and ran it through my hair. I regarded the sphinx.

". . . and goes round and round and round," it muttered.

I cleared my throat. No reaction. The beast was staring past me. I wondered whether I might simply be able to slip off . . .

No. The gaze shifted to me.

"Good morning," I said cheerfully.

There was a brief gnashing of teeth.

"All right," I said, "you've taken a lot longer than I did. If you haven't got it by now I don't care to play any longer."

"I don't like your riddle," it said at last.

"Sorry."

"What is the answer?"

"You're giving up?"

"I must. What is the answer?"

I raised a hand.

"Hold on," I said. "These things should be done in proper order. I should have the preferred answer to yours before I tell you mine."

It nodded.

"There is some justice in that. All right—the Keep of the Four Worlds."

"What?"

"That is the answer. The Keep of the Four Worlds."

I thought of Melman's words. "Why?" I asked.

"It lies at the crossroads of the worlds of the four elements, where it rises from the earth in flames, assailed by the winds and waters."

"What about the business of overseeing all things?"

"It could refer to the view, or to its master's imperialistic designs. Or both."

"Who is its master?"

"I don't know. That information is not essential to the answer."

"Where'd you pick up this riddle, anyhow?"

"From a traveler, a few months back."

"Why'd you choose this one, of all the riddles you must know, to ask me?"

"It stopped me, so it had to be good."

"What became of the traveler?"

"He went on his way, uneaten. He'd answered my riddle."

"He had a name?"

"He wouldn't say."

"Describe him, please."

"I can't. He was well muffled."

"And he said nothing more about the Keep of the Four Worlds?"

"No."

"Well," I said. "I believe I'll follow his example and take a walk myself."

I turned and faced the slope to my right.

"Wait!"

"What?" I asked.

"Your riddle," it stated. "I've given you the answer to mine. You must now tell me what it is that is green and red and goes round and round and round."

I glanced downward, scanned the ground. Oh, yes, there it was—my dumbbell-shaped stone. I took several steps and stood beside it.

"A frog in a Cuisinart," I said.

"What?"

Its shoulder muscles bunched, its eyes narrowed and its many teeth became very apparent. I spoke a few words to Frakir and felt her stir as I squatted and caught hold of the stone with my right hand.

"That's it," I said, rising. "It's one of those visual things—"

"That's a rotten riddle!" the sphinx announced.

With my left index finger I made two quick movements in the air before me.

"What are you doing?" it asked.

"Drawing lines from your ears to your eyes," I said.

Frakir became visible at about that moment, sliding from my left wrist to my hand, twining among my fingers. The sphinx's eyes darted in that direction. I raised the stone level with my right shoulder. One end of Frakir fell free and hung writhing from my extended hand. She began to brighten, then glowed like a hot silver wire.

"I believe the contest is a draw," I stated. "What do you think?"

The sphinx licked its lips.

"Yes," it finally said, sighing. "I suppose you are right."

"Then I will bid you good day," I said.

"Yes. Pity. Very well. Good day. But before you go may I have your name—for the record?"

"Why not?" I said. "I am Merlin, of Chaos."

"Ah," it said, "then someone would have come to avenge you."

"It's possible."

"Then a draw is indeed best. Go."

I backed farther off before turning and proceeding up the slope to my right. I remained on guard until I was out of that place, but there was no pursuit.

I began jogging. I was thirsty and hungry, but I wasn't likely to turn up breakfast in this desolate, rocky place under a lemon sky. Frakir recoiled and faded. I began drawing deep breaths as I headed away from the risen sun.

Wind in my hair, dust in my eyes . . . I bore toward a cluster of boulders, passed among them. Seen from amid their shadows the sky grew greenish above me. Emerging, I came upon a softer plain, glitters in the distance, a few clouds rising to my left.

I maintained a steady pace, reaching a small rise, mounting it, descending its farther side where sparse grasses waved. A grove of mop-topped trees in the distance . . . I headed for them, startling a small orange-furred creature that sprang across my path and tore away to the left. Moments later, a dark bird flashed by, uttering a wailing note, headed in the same direction. I ran on, and the sky continued to darken.

Green the sky and thicker the grasses, green the grasses, too . . . Heavy gusts of wind at irregular intervals . . . Nearer the trees . . . A singing sound emerges from their branches . . . The clouds sweep onward . . .

A tightness goes out of my muscles and a familiar fluidity enters . . . I pass the first tree, treading upon long, fallen leaves . . . I pass among hairy-barked boles . . . The way I follow is hard-packed, becomes a trail, strange foot marks cast within it . . . It drops, curves, widens, narrows again . . . The ground rises at either hand . . . the trees sound bass viol notes . . . Patches of sky amid the leaves are the color of Morinci turquoise . . . Streamers of cloud snake forward like silver rivers . . . Small clusters of blue flowers appear on the trail walls . . . The walls rise higher, passing above my head . . . The way grows rocky . . . I run on . . .

My path widens, widens, descending steadily . . . Even before I see or hear it, I smell the water . . . Carefully now, among the stones . . . A bit slower here . . . I turn and see the stream, high, rocky banks at either hand, a meter or two of shoreline before the rise . . .

Slower still, beside the gurgling, sparkling flow . . . To follow its meandering . . . Bends, curves, trees high overhead, exposed roots in the wall to my right, gray and yellow talus-fall along the flaky base . . .

My shelf widens, the walls lower . . . More sand and fewer rocks beneath my feet . . . Lowering, lowering . . . Head-height, shoulder-height . . . Another bending of the way, slope descending . . . Waist high . . . Green-leafed trees all about me, blue sky overhead, off to the right a hard-packed trail . . . I mount the slope, I follow it . . .

Trees and shrubs, bird notes and cool breeze . . . I suck the air, I lengthen my stride . . . I cross a wooden bridge, footfalls echoing, creek flowing to the now-masked stream, moss-grown boulders beside its cool . . . Low stone wall to my right now . . . Wagon ruts ahead . . .

Wildflowers at either hand . . . A sound of distant laughter, echoing . . . The neigh of a horse . . . Creak of a cart . . . Turn left . . . Widening of the way . . . Shadow and sunlight, shadow and sunlight . . . Dapple, dapple . . . River to the left, wider now, sparkling . . . Haze of smoke above the next hill . . .

I slow as I near the summit. I reach it walking, dusting my garments, brushing my hair into place, limbs tingling, lungs pumping, bands of perspiration cooling me. I spit grit. Below me and to the right lies a country inn, some tables on its wide, rough-hewn porch, facing the river, a few in a garden nearby. Bye-bye, present tense. I am arrived.

I walked on down and located a pump at the far side of the building, where I washed my face, hands and arms, my left forearm still sore and slightly inflamed where Jasra had attacked me. I made my way to the porch then and took a small table, after waving to a serving woman I saw within. After a time, she brought me porridge and sausages and eggs and bread and butter and strawberry preserves and tea.

I finished it all quickly and ordered another round of the same. The second time through a feeling of returning normalcy occurred, and I slowed and enjoyed it and watched the river go by.

It was a strange way to wind up the job. I had been looking forward to some leisurely travel, to a long lazy vacation, now my work had been done. The small matter of S had been all that stood in my way—a thing I had been certain I could settle quickly. Now I was in the middle of something I did not understand, something dangerous and bizarre. Sipping my tea and feeling the day warm about me, I could be lulled into a momentary sense of peace. But I knew it for a fleeting thing. There could be no true rest, no safety for me, until this matter was settled. Looking back over events, I saw that I could no longer trust my reactions alone for my deliverance, for a resolution of this affair. It was time to formulate a plan.

The identity of S and S's removal were high on my list of things that needed knowing and doing. Higher still was the determination of S's motive. My notion that I was dealing with a simple-minded psycho had dissolved. S was too well organized and possessed some very unusual abilities. I began searching my past for possible candidates. But though I could think of quite a few capable of managing what had occurred thus far, none of these were particularly ill-disposed toward me. However, Amber *had* been mentioned in that strange diary of Melman's. Theoretically, this made the whole thing a family matter and I suppose put me under some obligation to call it to the attention of the others. But to do so would be like asking for help, giving up, saying that I couldn't manage my own affairs. And threats on my life were my own affair. Julia was my affair. The vengeance on this one was to be mine. I had to think about it some more . . .

Ghostwheel?

I mulled it over, dismissed it, thought about it again. Ghostwheel . . . No. Untried. Still developing. The only reason it had occurred to me at all was because it was my pet,

my major accomplishment in life, my surprise for the others.
I was just looking for an easy way out. I would need a lot
more data to submit, which meant I had to go after it, of
course.

Ghostwheel . . .

Right now I needed more information. I had the cards
and the diary. I didn't want to fool with the Trumps any
more at this point, since the first one had seemed something
of a trap. I would go through the diary soon, though my
initial impression had been that it was too subjective to be
of much help. I ought to go back to Melman's for a final
look around, though, in case there was anything I had missed.
Then I ought to look up Luke and see whether he could tell
me anything more—even some small remark—that might
be of value. Yes . . .

I sighed and stretched. I watched the river a little longer
and finished my tea. I ran Frakir over a fistful of money
and selected sufficient transformed coinage to pay for my
meal. Then I returned to the road. Time to run on back.

CHAPTER 5

I came jogging up the street in the light of late afternoon and halted when I was abreast of my car. I'd almost failed to recognize it. It was covered with dust, ashes, and water stains. How long had I been away, anyhow? I hadn't tried to reckon the time differential between here and where I'd been, but my car looked as if it had been standing exposed for over a month. It seemed intact, though. It had not been vandalized and—

My gaze had drifted past the hood and on ahead. The building that had housed the Brutus Storage Company and the late Victor Melman no longer stood. A burnt-out, collapsed skeleton of the place occupied the corner, parts of two walls standing. I headed toward it.

Walking about it, I studied what was left. The charred remains of the place were cold and settled. Gray streaks and sooty fairy circles indicated that water had been pumped into it, had since evaporated. The ashy smell was not particularly strong.

Had I started it, with that fire in the bathtub? I wondered. I didn't think so. Mine had been a small enough blaze, and

56

well confined, with no indication of its spreading while I was waiting.

A boy on a green bicycle pedaled past while I was studying the ruin. Several minutes later he returned and halted about ten feet from me. He looked to be about ten years old.

"I saw it," he announced. "I saw it burn."

"When was that?" I asked him.

"Three days ago."

"They know how it started?"

"Something in the storage place, something flam—"

"Flammable?"

"Yeah," he said through a gap-toothed smile. "Maybe on purpose. Something about insurance."

"Really?"

"Uh-huh. My dad said maybe business was bad."

"It's been known to happen," I said. "Was anybody hurt in the fire?"

"They thought maybe the artist who lived upstairs got burned up because nobody could find him. But they didn't see any bones or anything like that. It was a good fire. Burned a long time."

"Was it nighttime or daytime?"

"Nighttime. I watched from over there." He pointed to a place across the street and back in the direction from which I had come. "They put a lot of water on it."

"Did you see anyone come out of the building?"

"No," he said. "I got here after it was burning pretty good."

I nodded and turned back toward my car.

"You'd think bullets would explode in all that fire, wouldn't you?" he said.

"Yes," I answered.

"But they didn't."

I turned back.

"What do you mean?" I asked.

He was already digging in a pocket.

"Me and some of my friends were playing around in

there yesterday," he explained, "and we found a mess of
bullets."

He opened his hand to display several metallic objects.

As I moved toward him, he squatted and placed one of
the cylinders on the sidewalk. He reached out suddenly,
picked up a nearby rock and swung it toward it.

"Don't!" I cried.

The rock struck the shell and nothing happened.

"You could get hurt that way—" I began, but he interrupted.

"Naw. No way these suckers will explode. You can't
even set that pink stuff on fire. Got a match?"

"Pink stuff?" I said as he moved the rock to reveal a
mashed shell casing and a small trailing of pink powder.

"That," he said, pointing. "Funny, huh? I thought gunpowder was gray."

I knelt and touched the substance. I rubbed it between
my fingers. I sniffed it. I even tasted it. I couldn't tell what
the hell it was.

"Beats me," I told him. "Won't even burn, you say?"

"Nope. We put some on a newspaper and set the paper
on fire. It'll melt and run, that's all."

"You got a couple of extras?"

"Well . . . yeah."

"I'll give you a buck for them," I said.

He showed me his teeth and spaces again as his hand
vanished into the side of his jeans. I ran Frakir over some
odd Shadow cash and withdrew a dollar from the pile. He
handed me two sootstreaked double 30's as he accepted it.

"Thanks," he said.

"My pleasure. Anything else interesting in there?"

"Nope. All the rest is ashes."

I got into my car and drove. I ran it through the first car
wash I came to, since the wipers had only smeared the crap
on the windshield. As the rubbery tentacles slapped at me
through a sea of foam, I checked to see whether I still had

the matchbook Luke had given me. I did. Good. I'd seen a pay phone outside.

"Hello. New Line Motel," a young, male voice answered.

"You had a Lucas Raynard registered there a couple of days ago," I said. "I want to know whether he left a message for me. My name's Merle Corey."

"Just a minute."

Pause. Shuffle.

Then: "Yes, he did."

"What does it say?"

"It's in a sealed envelope. I'd rather not—"

"Okay. I'll come by."

I drove over. I located the man matching the voice at the desk in the lobby. I identified myself and claimed the envelope. The clerk—a slight, blond fellow with a bristly mustache—stared for a moment, then: "Are you going to see Mr. Raynard?"

"Yes."

He opened a drawer and withdrew a small brown envelope, its sides distended. Luke's name and room number were written on it.

"He didn't leave a forwarding address," he explained, opening the envelope, "and the maid found this ring on the bathroom counter after he'd checked out. Would you give it to him?"

"Sure," I said, and he passed it to me.

I seated myself in a lounge area off to the left. The ring was of pink gold and sported a blue stone. I couldn't recall ever having seen him wear it. I slipped it on the ring finger of my left hand and it fit perfectly. I decided to wear it until I could give it to him.

I opened the letter, written on motel stationery, and read:

Merle,
Too bad about dinner. I did wait around. Hope every-thing's okay. I'm leaving in the morning for Albu-querque. I'll be there three days. Then up to Santa Fe for three more. Staying at the Hilton in both towns.

I did have some more things I wanted to talk about.
Please get in touch.

                                              Luke

Hm.

I phoned my travel agent and discovered that I could be
on an afternoon flight to Albuquerque if I hustled. In that
I wanted a face-to-face rather than a phone talk, I did that
thing. I stopped by the office, picked up my ticket, paid
cash for it, drove to the airport and said good-bye to my
car as I parked it. I doubted I would ever see it again. I
hefted my backpack and walked to the terminal.

The rest was smooth and easy. As I watched the ground
drop away beneath me, I knew that a phase of my existence
had indeed ended. Like so many things, it was not at all
the way I had wanted it to be. I'd thought to wind up the
matter of S pretty quickly or else decide to forget about it,
and then visit people I'd been meaning to see for some time
and stop at a few places I'd long been curious about. Then
I would take off through Shadow for a final check on Ghostwheel, heading back to the brighter pole of my existence
after that. Now, my priorities had been shuffled—all because
S and Julia's death were somehow connected, and because
it involved a power from elsewhere in Shadow that I did
not understand.

It was the latter consideration that troubled me most. Was
I digging my grave as well as jeopardizing friends and
relatives because of my pride? I wanted to handle this myself,
friendly skies, but the more I thought about it the more
impressed I became with the adversary powers I had encountered and the paucity of my knowledge concerning S. It
wasn't fair not to let the others know—not if they might
be in danger, too. I'd love to wrap the whole thing up by
myself and give it to them for a present. Maybe I would,
too, but—

Damn it. I *had* to tell them. If S got me and turned on
them, they needed to know. If it were a part of something

larger, they needed to know. As much as I disliked the idea, I would have to tell them.

I leaned forward and my hand hovered above my backpack beneath the seat in front of me. It wouldn't hurt, I decided, to wait until after I'd spoken with Luke. I was out of town and probably safe now. There was the possibility of picking up a clue or two from Luke. I'd rather have more to give them when I told my story. I'd wait a little longer.

I sighed. I got a drink from the stewardess and sipped it. Driving to Albuquerque in a normal fashion would have taken too long. Short-cutting through Shadow would not work, because I'd never been there before and didn't know how to find the place. Too bad. I'd like to have my car there. Luke was probably in Santa Fe by now.

I sipped and I looked for shapes in the clouds. The things I found matched my mood, so I got out my paperback and read until we began our descent. When I looked again ranks of mountains filled my prospect for a time. A crackly voice assured me that the weather was pleasant. I wondered about my father.

I hiked in from my gate, passed a gift shop full of Indian jewelry, Mexican pots, and gaudy souvenirs, located a telephone, and called the local Hilton. Luke had already checked out, I learned. I phoned the Hilton in Santa Fe then. He had checked in there but was not in his room when they rang it for me. I made a reservation for myself and hung up. A woman at an information counter told me that I could catch a Shuttlejack to Santa Fe in about half an hour and sent me in the proper direction to buy a ticket. Santa Fe is one of the few state capitals without a major airport, I'd read somewhere.

While we were heading north on I-25, somewhere among lengthening shadows in the vicinity of Sandia Peak, Frakir tightened slightly upon my wrist and released the pressure a moment later. Again. Then once again. I glanced quickly about the small bus, seeking the danger against which I had just been warned.

I was seated in the rear of the vehicle. Up near the front was a middle-aged couple, speaking with Texas accents, wearing an ostentatious quantity of turquoise and silver jewelry; near the middle were three older women, talking about things back in New York; across the aisle from them was a young couple, very absorbed in each other; two young men with tennis racquets sat diagonally to the rear of them, talking about college; behind them was a nun, reading. I looked out the window again and saw nothing particularly threatening on the highway or near it. I did not want to draw to myself the attention that any location practices would involve either.

So I spoke a single word in Thari as I rubbed my wrist, and the warnings ceased. Even though the rest of the ride was uneventful, it bothered me, though an occasional false warning was possible just because of the nature of nervous systems. As I watched red shale and red and yellow earth streak by, bridged arroyos, viewed distant mountains and nearer slopes dotted with piñon, I wondered. S? Is S back there somewhere, somehow, watching, waiting? And if so, why? Couldn't we just sit down and talk about it over a couple of beers? Maybe it was based on some sort of mis-understanding.

I'd a feeling it was not a misunderstanding. But I'd settle for just knowing what was going on, even if nothing were resolved. I'd even pay for the beers.

The light of the setting sun touched flashes of brightness from streaks of snow in the Sangre de Cristos as we pulled into town; shadows slid across gray-green slopes; most of the buildings in sight were stuccoed. It felt about ten degrees cooler when I stepped down from the bus in front of the Hilton than it had when I'd boarded in Albuquerque. But then, I'd gained about two thousand feet in altitude and it was an hour and a quarter further along in the direction of evening.

I registered and found my room. I tried phoning Luke, but there was no answer. I showered then and changed into my spare outfit. Rang his room once more then, but still no answer. I was getting hungry and I'd hoped to have dinner with him.

I decided to find the bar and nurse a beer for a while, then try again. I hoped he didn't have a heavy date.

A Mr. Brazda, whom I approached in the lobby and asked for directions, turned out to be the manager. He asked about my room, we exchanged a few pleasantries and he showed me the corridor leading off to the lounge. I started in that direction, but didn't quite make it.

"Merle! What the hell are you doing here?" came a familiar voice.

I turned and regarded Luke, who had just entered the lobby. Sweaty and smiling, he was wearing dusty fatigues and boots, a fatigue cap, and a few streaks of grime. We shook hands and I said, "I wanted to talk to you." Then: "What'd you do, enlist in something?"

"No, I've been off hiking in the Pecos all day," he answered. "I always do that when I'm out this way. It's great."

"I'll have to try it sometime," I said. "Now it seems it's my turn to buy dinner."

"You're right," he answered. "Let me catch a shower and change clothes. I'll meet you in the bar in fifteen, twenty minutes. Okay?"

"Right. See you."

I headed up the corridor and located the place. It was medium-sized, dim, cool and relatively crowded, divided into two widely connected rooms, with low, comfortable-looking chairs and small tables.

A young couple was just abandoning a corner table off to my left, drinks in hand, to follow a waitress into the adjacent dining room. I took the table. A little later a cocktail waitress came by, and I ordered a beer.

Sitting there, several minutes later, sipping, and letting my mind drift over the perversely plotted events of the past several days, I realized that one of the place's passing figures had failed to pass. It had come to a halt at my side—just far enough to the rear to register only as a dark peripheral presence.

It spoke softly: "Excuse me. May I ask you a question?"

I turned my head, to behold a short, thin man of Spanish appearance, his hair and mustache flecked with gray. He was sufficiently well dressed and groomed to seem a local business type. I noted a chipped front tooth when he smiled so briefly—just a twitch—as to indicate nervousness.

"My name's Dan Martinez," he said, not offering to shake hands. He glanced at the chair across from me. "Could I sit down a minute?"

"What's this about? If you're selling something, I'm not interested. I'm waiting for somebody and—"

He shook his head.

"No, nothing like that. I know you're waiting for someone—a Mr. Lucas Raynard. It involves him, actually."

I gestured at the chair.

"Okay. Sit down and ask your question."

He did so, clasping his hands and placing them on the table between us. He leaned forward.

"I overheard you talking in the lobby," he began, "and I got the impression you knew him fairly well. Would you mind telling me for about how long you've known him?"

"If that's all you want to know," I answered, "for about eight years. We went to college together, and we worked for the same company for several years after that."

"Grand Design," he stated, "the San Francisco computer firm. Didn't know him before college, huh?"

"It seems you already know quite a bit," I said. "What did you want, anyway? Are you some kind of cop?"

"No," he said, "nothing like that. I assure you I'm not trying to get your friend into trouble. I am simply trying to save myself some. Let me just ask you—"

I shook my head.

"No more freebies," I told him. "I don't care to talk to strangers about my friends without some pretty good reasons."

He unclasped his hands and spread them wide.

"I'm not being underhanded," he said, "when I know you'll tell him about it. In fact, I want you to. He knows me. I want him to know I'm asking around about him, okay? It'll actually be to his benefit. Hell, I'm even asking a friend, aren't I? Someone who might be willing to lie to help him out. And I just need a couple simple facts—"

"And I just need one simple reason: why do you want this information?"

He sighed. "Okay," he said. "He offered me—tentatively, mind you—a very interesting investment opportunity. It would involve a large sum of money. There is an element of risk, as in most ventures involving new companies in a highly competitive area, but the possible returns do make it tempting."

I nodded.

"And you want to know whether he's honest."

He chuckled. "I don't really care whether he's honest," he said. "My only concern is whether he can deliver a product with no strings on it."

Something about the way this man talked reminded me of someone. I tried, but couldn't recall who it was.

"Ah," I said, taking a sip of beer. "I'm slow today. Sorry. Of course this deal involves computers."

"Of course."

"You want to know whether his present employer can nail him if he goes into business out here with whatever he's bringing with him."

"In a word, yes."

"I give up," I said. "It would take a better man than me to answer that. Intellectual properties represent a tricky area of the law. I don't know what he's selling and I don't know where it comes from—he gets around a lot. But even if I did know, I have no idea what your legal position would be."

"I didn't expect anything beyond that," he said, smiling.

I smiled back.

"So you've sent your message," I said.

He nodded and began to rise.

"Oh, just one thing more," he began.

"Yes?"

"Did he ever mention places," he said, staring full into my eyes, "called Amber or the Courts of Chaos?"

He could not have failed to note my startled reaction, which had to have given him a completely false impression. I was sure that he was sure I was lying when I answered him truthfully.

"No, I never heard him refer to them. Why do you ask?"

He shook his head as he pushed his chair back and stepped away from the table. He was smiling again.

"It's not important. Thank you, Mr. Corey. *Nus a dhab-zhun dhuilsha.*"

He practically fled around the corner.

"Wait!" I called out, so loudly that there was a moment of silence and heads turned in my direction.

I got to my feet and started after him, when I heard my name called.

"Hey, Merle! Don't run off! I'm here already!"

I turned. Luke had just come in through the entrance behind me, hair still shower-damp. He advanced, clapped me on the shoulder, and lowered himself into the seat Martinez had just vacated. He nodded at my half-finished beer as I sat down again.

"I need one of those," he said. "Lord, am I thirsty!" Then, "Where were you off to when I came in?"

I found myself reluctant to describe my recent encounter, not least because of its strange conclusion. Apparently, he had just missed seeing Martinez.

So: "I was heading for the john."

"It's back that way," he told me, nodding in the direction from which he had entered. "I passed it on the way in."

His eyes shifted downward.

"Say, that ring you have on—"

"Oh, yeah," I said. "You left it at the New Line Motel. I picked it up for you when I collected your message. Here, let me . . ."

I tugged at it, but it wouldn't come off.

"Seems to be stuck," I noted. "Funny. It went on easy enough."

"Maybe your finger's swollen," he remarked. "It could have something to do with the altitude. We're up pretty high."

He caught the waitress's attention and ordered a beer, while I kept twisting at the ring.

"Guess I'll just have to sell it to you," he said. "Give you a good deal."

"We'll see," I told him. "Back in a minute."

He raised one hand limply and let it fall as I headed toward the rest room.

There was no one else in the facility, and so I spoke the words that released Frakir from the suppression spell I had uttered back aboard the Shuttlejack. There followed immediate movement. Before I could issue another command, Frakir became shimmeringly visible in the act of uncoiling, crept across the back of my hand and wound about my ring finger. I watched, fascinated, as the finger darkened and began to ache beneath a steady tightening.

A loosening followed quickly, leaving my finger looking as if it had been threaded. I got the idea. I unscrewed the ring along the track that had been pressed into my flesh. Frakir moved again as if to snag it and I stroked her.

"Okay," I said. "Thanks. Return."

There seemed a moment of hesitation, but my will proved sufficient without a more formal command. She retreated back across my hand, rewound herself about my wrist, and faded.

I finished up in there and returned to the bar. I passed Luke his ring as I seated myself, and took a sip of beer.

"How'd you get it off?" he asked.

"A bit of soap," I answered.

He wrapped it in his handkerchief and put it in his pocket.

"Guess I can't take your money for it, then."

"Guess not. Aren't you going to wear it?"

"No, it's a present. You know, I hardly expected you to make the scene here," he commented, scooping a handful of peanuts from a bowl that had appeared in my absence. "I thought maybe you'd just call when you got my message, and we could set something up for later. Glad you did, though. Who knows when later might have been. See, I had some plans that started moving faster than I'd thought they would—and that's what I wanted to talk to you about."

I nodded.

"I had a few things I wanted to talk to you about, too." He returned my nod.

I had decided back in the lavatory definitely to refrain from mentioning Martinez yet, and the first things he had said and implied. Although the entire setup did not sound as if it involved anything in which I had any interest any longer, I always feel more secure in talking with anyone— even friends—when I have at least a little special information they don't know I have. So I decided to keep it that way for now.

"So let's be civilized and hold everything important till after dinner," he said, slowly shredding his napkin and wadding the pieces, "and go somewhere we can talk in private then."

"Good idea," I agreed. "Want to eat here?"

He shook his head.

"I've been eating here. It's good, but I want a change. I had my heart set on eating at a place around the corner. Let me go and see if they've got a table."

"Okay."

He gulped the rest of his drink and departed.

. . . And then the mention of Amber. Who the hell was Martinez? It was more than a little necessary that I learn this, because it was obvious to me that he was something other than he appeared to be. His final words had been in Thari, my native tongue. How this could be and why it should be, I had no idea. I cursed my own inertia, at having let the S situation slide for so long. It was purely a result of my arrogance. I'd never anticipated the convoluted mess the affair would become. Served me right, though I didn't appreciate the service.

"Okay," Luke said, rounding the corner, digging into his pocket, and tossing some money on the table. "We've got a reservation. Drink up, and let's take a walk."

I finished, stood and followed him. He led me through the corridors and back to the lobby, then out and along a hallway to the rear. We emerged into a balmy evening and crossed the parking lot to the sidewalk that ran along Guadaloupe Street. From there it was only a short distance to the place where it intersected with Alameda. We crossed twice there and strolled on past a big church, then turned right at the next corner. Luke pointed out a restaurant called La Tertulia across the street a short distance ahead.

"There," he said.

We crossed over and found our way to the entrance. It was a low adobe building, Spanish, venerable, and somewhat elegant inside. We went through a pitcher of sangria, orders of pollo adova, bread puddings, and many cups of coffee, keeping our agreement not to speak of anything serious during dinner.

During the course of the meal Luke was greeted twice, by different guys passing through the room, both of whom paused at the table to pass a few pleasantries.

"You know everybody in this town?" I asked him a bit later.

He chuckled. "I do a lot of business here."

"Really? It seems a pretty small town."

"Yes, but that's deceptive. It *is* the state capital. There're a lot of people here buying what we're selling."

"So you're out this way a lot?"

He nodded. "It's one of the hottest spots on my circuit."

"How do you manage all this business when you're out hiking in the woods?"

He looked up from the small battle formation he was creating from the things on the table. He smiled.

"I've got to have a little recreation," he said. "I get tired of cities and offices. I have to get away and hike around, or canoe or kayak or something like that—or I'd go out of my gourd. In fact, that's one of the reasons I built up the business in this town—quick access to a lot of good places for that stuff."

He took a drink of coffee.

"You know," he continued, "it's such a nice night we ought to take a drive, let you get a feeling of what I mean."

"Sounds good," I said, stretching my shoulders and looking for our waiter. "But isn't it too dark to see much?"

"No. The moon'll be up, the stars are out, the air's real clear. You'll see."

I got the tab, paid up, and we strolled out. Sure enough, the moon had risen.

"Car's in the hotel lot," he said as we hit the street. "This side."

He indicated a station wagon once we were back in the parking lot, unlocked it, and waved me aboard. He drove us out, turned at the nearest corner, and followed the Alameda to the Paseo, took a right leading uphill on a street called Otero and another onto Hyde Park Road. From then on traffic was very light. We passed a sign indicating that we were heading toward a ski basin.

As we worked our way through many curves, heading generally upward, I felt a certain tension going out of me. Soon we had left all signs of habitation behind us, and the night and the quiet settled fully. No streetlights here. Through the opened window I smelled pine trees. The air was cool. I rested, away from S and everything else.

I glanced at Luke. He stared straight ahead, brow furrowed. He felt my gaze, though, because he seemed to relax suddenly and he shot me a grin.

"Who goes first?" he asked.

"Go ahead," I answered.

"Okay. When we were talking the other morning about your leaving Grand D, you said you weren't going to work anywhere else and you weren't planning on teaching."

"That's right."

"You said you were just going to travel around."

"Yep."

"Something else did suggest itself to me a little later on."

I remained silent as he glanced my way.

"I was wondering," he said after a time, "whether you might not be shopping around—either for backing in getting your own company going, or for a buyer for something you have to sell. You know what I mean?"

"You think I came up with something—innovative—and didn't want Grand Design to have it."

He slapped the seat beside him.

"Always knew you were no fool," he said. "So you're screwing around now, to allow decent time for its development. Then you hunt up the buyer with the most bread."

"Makes sense," I said, "if that were the case. But it isn't."

He chuckled.

"It's okay," he said. "Just because I work for Grand D doesn't make me their fink. You ought to know that."

"I do know it."

"And I wasn't asking just to pry. In fact, I had other intentions completely. I'd like to see you make out with it, make out big."

"Thanks."

"I might even be of some assistance—valuable assistance—in the matter."

"I begin to get the drift, Luke, but—"

"Just hear me out, huh? But answer one thing first, though, if you would: You haven't signed anything with anybody in the area, have you?"

"No."

"Didn't think so. It would seem a little premature."

The roadside trees were larger now, the night breeze a bit more chill. The moon seemed bigger, more brilliant up here than it had in the town below. We rounded several more curves, eventually commencing a long series of switchbacks that bore us higher and higher. I caught occasional glimpses of sharp drops to the left. There was no guard rail.

"Look," he said, "I'm not trying to cut myself in for nothing. I'm not asking you for a piece of the action for old times' sake or anything like that. That's one thing and business is another—though it never hurts to do a deal with someone you know you can trust. Let me tell you some of the facts of life. If you've got some really fantastic design, sure, you can go sell it for a bundle to lots of people in the business—if you're careful, damn careful. But that's it. Your golden opportunity's flown then. If you really want to clean up, you start your own outfit. Look at Apple. If it really catches on you can always sell out then, for a lot more than you'd get from just peddling the idea. You may be a whiz at design, but I know the marketplace. And I know people—all over the country—people who'd trust me enough to bankroll us to see it off the ground and out on the street. Shit! I'm not going to stay with Grand D all my life. Let me in and I'll get us the financing. You run the shop and I'll run the business. That's the only way to go with something big."

"Oh, my," I sighed. "Man, it actually sounds nice. But you're following a bum scent. I don't have anything to sell."

"Come on!" he said. "You know you can level with me. Even if you absolutely refuse to go that way, I'm not going to talk about it. I don't screw my buddies. I just think you're making a mistake if you don't develop it yourself."

"Luke, I meant what I said."

He was silent for a little while. Then I felt his gaze upon me again. When I glanced his way I saw that he was smiling.

"What," I asked him, "is the next question?"

"What is Ghostwheel?" he said.

"What?"

"Top secret, hush-hush, Merle Corey project. Ghost-wheel," he answered. "Computer design incorporating shit nobody's ever seen before. Liquid semiconductors, cryo-genic tanks, plasma—"

I started laughing.

"My God!" I said. "It's a joke, that's what it is. Just a crazy hobby thing. It was a design game—a machine that could never be built on Earth. Well, maybe most of it could. But it wouldn't function. It's like an Escher drawing—looks great on paper, but it can't be done in real life." Then after a moment's reflection, I asked, "How is it you even know about it? I've never mentioned it to anyone."

He cleared his throat as he took another turn. The moon was raked by treetops. A few beads of moisture appeared upon the windshield.

"Well, you weren't all that secret about it," he answered. "There were designs and graphs and notes all over your work table and drawing board any number of times I was at your place. I could hardly help but notice. Most of them were even labeled 'Ghostwheel.' And nothing anything like it ever showed up at Grand D, so I simply assumed it was your pet project and your ticket to security. You never impressed me as the impractical dreamer type. Are you sure you're giving this to me straight?"

"If we were to sit down and build as much as could be constructed of that thing right here," I replied honestly, "it would just sit there and look weird and wouldn't do a damned thing."

He shook his head.

"That sounds perverse," he said. "It's not like you, Merle. Why the hell would you waste your time designing a machine that doesn't function?"

"It was an exercise in design theory—" I began.

"Excuse me, but that sounds like bullshit," he said. "You mean to say there's no place in the universe that damn machine of yours would kick over?"

"I didn't say that. I was trying to explain that I designed it to operate under bizarre hypothetical conditions."

"Oh. In other words, if I find a place like that on another world we can clean up?"

"Uh, yeah."

"You're weird, Merle. You know that?"

"Uh-huh."

"Another dream shot to shit. Oh, well . . . Say, is there anything unusual about it that could be adapted to the here and now?"

"Nope. It couldn't perform its functions here."

"What's so special about its functions, anyhow?"

"A lot of theoretical crap involving space and time and some notions of some guys named Everett and Wheeler. It's only amenable to a mathematical explanation."

"You sure?"

"What difference does it make, anyhow? I've got no product, we've got no company. Sorry. Tell Martinez and associates it was a blind alley."

"Huh? Who's Martinez?"

"One of your potential investors in Corey and Raynard, Inc.," I said. "Dan Martinez—middle-aged, a bit short, kind of distinguished-looking, chipped front tooth..."

His brow furrowed. "Merle, I don't know who the hell you're talking about."

"He came up to me while I was waiting for you in the bar. Seemed to know an awful lot about you. Started asking questions on what I can now see as the potential situation you just described. Acted as if you'd approached him to invest in the thing."

"Uh-uh," he said. "I don't know him. How come you didn't tell me sooner?"

"He beat it, and you said no business till after dinner. Didn't seem all that important, anyway. He even as much as asked me to let you know he'd been inquiring about you."

"What, specifically, did he want to know?"

"Whether you could deliver an unencumbered computer property and keep the investors out of court, was what I gathered."

He slapped the wheel. "This makes no sense at all," he said. "It really doesn't."

"It occurs to me that he might have been hired to investigate a bit—or even just to shake you up some and keep you honest—by the people you've been sounding out to invest in this thing."

"Merle, do you think I'm so damn stupid I'd waste a lot of time digging up investors before I was even sure there was something to put the money into? I haven't talked to anybody about this except you, and I guess I won't be now either. Who do you think he could have been? What did he want?"

I shook my head, but I was remembering those words in Thari.

Why not?

"He also asked me whether I'd ever heard you refer to a place called Amber."

He was looking in the rearview mirror when I said it, and he jerked the wheel to catch a sudden curve.

"Amber? You're kidding."

"No."

"Strange. It has to be a coincidence—"

"What?"

"I did hear a reference to a kind of dreamland place called Amber, last week. But I never mentioned it to anybody. It was just drunken babbling."

"Who? Who said it?"

"A painter I know. A real nut, but a very talented guy. Name's Melman. I like his work a lot, and I've bought several of his paintings. I'd stopped by to see whether he had anything new this last time I was in town. He didn't, but I stayed pretty late at his place anyway, talking and drinking and smoking some stuff he had. He got pretty high after a while and he started talking about magic. Not card tricks, I mean. Ritual stuff, you know?"

"Yes."

"Well, after a time he started doing some of it. If it weren't that I was kind of stoned myself I'd swear that it worked—that he levitated, summoned sheets of fire, conjured and banished a number of monsters. There had to've been acid in something he gave me. But damn! It sure seemed real."

"Uh-huh."

"Anyway," he went on, "he mentioned a sort of archetypal city. I couldn't tell whether it sounded more like Sodom and Gomorrah or Camelot—all the adjectives he used. He called the place Amber, and said that it was run by a half-mad family, with the city itself peopled by their bastards and folks whose ancestors they'd brought in from other places ages ago. Shadows of the family and the city supposedly figure in most major legends and such—whatever that means. I could never be sure whether he was talking in metaphor, which he did a lot, or just what the hell he meant. But that's where I heard the place mentioned."

"Interesting," I said. "Melman is dead. His place burned down a few days ago."

"No, I didn't know." He glanced into the mirror again. "Did you know him?"

"I met him—after you left this last time. Kinsky told me Julia'd been seeing him, and I looked the guy up to see what he could tell me about her. You see—well, Julia's dead."

"How'd it happen? I just saw her last week."

"In a very bizarre fashion. She was killed by a strange animal."

"Lord!"

He braked suddenly and pulled off the road onto a wide shoulder to the left. It looked upon a steep, tree-filled drop. Above the trees I could see the tiny lights of the city across a great distance.

He killed the engine and the headlights. He took a Durham's bag from his pocket and began rolling a cigarette. I caught him glancing upward and ahead.

"You've been checking that mirror a lot."

"Yes," he replied. "I was just about sure a car had been following us all the way from the parking lot down at the Hilton. It was a few turns behind us for the longest while. Now it seems to have disappeared."

He lit his cigarette and opened the door.

"Let's get some air."

I followed him and we stood for a few moments staring out across the big spaces, the moonlight strong enough to cast the shadows of some trees near to us. He threw down the cigarette and stamped on it.

"Shit!" he said. "This is getting too involved! I knew

Julia was seeing Melman, okay? I went to see her the night after I'd seen him, okay? I even delivered a small parcel he'd asked me to take her, okay?"

"Cards," I said.

He nodded.

I withdrew them from my pocket and held them toward him. He barely glanced at them there in the dim light, but he nodded again.

"Those cards," he said. Then: "You still liked her, didn't you?"

"Yes, I guess I did."

"Oh, hell," he sighed. "All right. There are some things I'm going to have to tell you, old buddy. Not all of them nice. Give me just a minute to sort it all out. You've just given me one big problem—or I've given it to myself, because I've just decided something."

He kicked a patch of gravel and the stones rattled down the hillside.

"Okay," he said. "First, give me those cards."

"Why?"

"I'm going to tear them into confetti."

"The hell you are. Why?"

"They're dangerous."

"I already know that. I'll hang onto them."

"You don't understand."

"So explain."

"It's not that easy. I have to decide what to tell you and what not to."

"Why not just tell me everything?"

"I can't. Believe me—"

I hit the ground as soon as I heard the first shot, which ricocheted off a boulder to our right. Luke didn't. He began running in a zigzag pattern toward a cluster of trees off to our left, from which two more shots were fired. He had something in his hand and he raised it.

Luke fired three times. Our assailant got off one more round. After Luke's second shot I heard someone gasp. I was on my feet by then and running toward him, a rock in my hand. After his third shot I heard a body fall.

I reached him just as he was turning the body over, in time to see what seemed a faint cloud of blue or gray mist emerge from the man's mouth past his chipped tooth and drift away.

"What the hell was that?" Luke asked as it blew away.

"You saw it, too? I don't know."

He looked down at the limp form with the dark spot growing larger on its shirtfront, a .38 revolver still clutched in the right hand.

"I didn't know you carried a gun," I said.

"When you're on the road as much as I am, you go heeled," he answered. "I pick up a new one in each city I hit and sell it when I leave. Airline security. Guess I won't be selling this one. I never saw this guy, Merle. You?"

I nodded.

"That's Dan Martinez, the man I was telling you about."

"Oh, boy," he said. "Another damn complication. Maybe I should just join a Zen monastery someplace and persuade myself it doesn't matter. I—"

Suddenly, he raised his left fingertips to his forehead.

"Oh-oh," he said then. "Merle, the keys are in the ignition. Get in the car and drive back to the hotel right away. Leave me here. Hurry!"

"What's going on? What—"

He raised his weapon, a snub-nosed automatic, and pointed it at me.

"Now! Shut up and go!"

"But—"

He lowered the muzzle and put a bullet into the ground between my feet. Then he aimed it squarely at my abdomen.

"Merlin, son of Corwin," he said through clenched teeth, "if you don't start running right now you're a dead man!"

I followed his advice, raising a shower of gravel and laying some streaks of rubber coming out of the U-turn I spun the wagon through. I roared down the hill and skidded around the curve to my right. I braked for the next one to my left. Then I slowed.

I pulled off to the left, at the foot of a bluff, near some shrubbery. I killed the engine and the lights and put on the parking brake. I opened the door quietly and did not close it fully after I'd slipped out. Sounds carry too well in places like this.

I started back, keeping to the darker, righthand side of the road. It was very quiet. I rounded the first turn and headed for the next one. Something flew from one tree to another. An owl, I think. I moved more slowly than I wanted to, for the sake of silence, as I neared the second turning.

I made my way around that final corner on all fours, taking advantage of the cover provided by rocks and foliage. I halted then and studied the area we had occupied. Nothing in sight. I advanced slowly, cautiously, ready to freeze, drop, dive, or spring up into a run as the situation required.

Nothing stirred, save branches in the wind. No one in sight.

I rose into a crouch and continued, still more slowly, still hugging the cover.

Not there. He had taken off for somewhere. I moved nearer, halted again and listened for at least a minute. No sounds betrayed any moving presences.

I crossed to the place where Martinez had fallen. The body was gone. I paced about the area but could locate nothing to give me any sort of clue as to what might have occurred following my departure. I could think of no reason for calling out, so I didn't.

I walked back to the car without misadventure, got in and headed for town. I couldn't even speculate as to what the hell was going on.

I left the wagon in the hotel lot, near to the spot where it had been parked earlier. Then I went inside, walked to Luke's room, and knocked on the door. I didn't really expect a response, but it seemed the proper thing to do preparatory to breaking and entering.

I was careful to snap only the lock, leaving the door and the fame intact, because Mr. Brazda had seemed a nice guy. It took a little longer, but there was no one in sight. I reached in and turned on the light, did a quick survey, then slipped inside quickly. I stood listening for a few minutes but heard no sounds of activity from the hall.

Tight ship. Suitcase on luggage rack, empty. Clothing hung in closet—nothing in the pockets except for two matchbooks, and a pen and pencil. A few other garments and some undergarments in a drawer, nothing with them. Toiletries in shaving kit or neatly arrayed on countertop. Nothing peculiar there. A copy of B. H. Liddell Hart's *Strategy* lay upon the bedside table, a bookmark about three-quarters of the way into it.

His fatigues had been thrown onto a chair, his dusty boots stood next to it, socks beside them. Nothing inside the boots but a pair of blousing bands. I checked the shirt pockets, which at first seemed empty, but my fingertips then discovered a number of small white paper pellets in one of them. Puzzled, I unfolded a few. Bizarre secret messages? No . . . No sense getting completely paranoid, when a few brown flecks on a paper answered the question. Tobacco. They were pieces of cigarette paper. Obviously he stripped his butts when he was hiking in the wilderness. I recalled a few past hikes with him. He hadn't always been that neat.

I went through the trousers. There was a damp bandana in one hip pocket and a comb in the other. Nothing in the right front pocket, a single round of ammo in the left. On an impulse, I pocketed the shell, then went on to look beneath the mattress and behind the drawers. I even looked in the toilet's flush box. Nothing. Nothing to explain his strange behavior.

Leaving the car keys on the bedside table I departed and returned to my own room. I did not care that he'd know I'd broken in. In fact, I rather liked the idea. It irritated me that he'd poked around in my Ghostwheel papers. Besides, he owed me a damned good explanation for his behavior on the mountain.

I undressed, showered, got into bed, and doused my light. I'd have left him a note, too, except that I don't like to create evidence and I had a strong feeling that he wouldn't be coming back.

CHAPTER 6

He was a short, heavy-set man with a somewhat florid complexion, his dark hair streaked with white and perhaps a bit thin on top. I sat in the study of his semirural home in upstate New York, sipping a beer and telling him my troubles. It was a breezy, star-dotted night beyond the window and he was a good listener.

"You say that Luke didn't show up the following day," he said. "Did he send a message?"

"No."

"What exactly did you do that day?"

"I checked his room in the morning. It was just as I'd left it. I went by the desk. Nothing, like I said. Then I had breakfast and I checked again. Nothing again. So I took a long walk around the town. Got back a little after noon, had lunch, and tried the room again. It was the same. I borrowed the car keys then and drove back up to the place we'd been the night before. No sign of anything unusual there, looking at it in the light of day. I even climbed down the slope and hunted around. No body, no clues. I drove back, replaced the keys, hung around the hotel till dinner-time, ate, then called you. After you told me to come on up, I made a reservation and went to bed early. Caught the Shuttlejack this morning and flew here from Albuquerque."

"And you checked again this morning?"

"Yeah. Nothing new."

He shook his head and relit his pipe.

His name was Bill Roth, and he had been my father's friend as well as his attorney, back when he'd lived in this area. He was possibly the only man on Earth Dad had trusted, and I trusted him, too. I'd visited him a number of times during my eight years—most recently, unhappily, a year and a half earlier, at the time of his wife, Alice's, funeral. I had told him my father's story, as I had heard it from his own lips, outside the Courts of Chaos, because I'd gotten the impression that he had wanted Bill to know what had been going on, felt he'd owed him some sort of explanation for all the help he'd given him. And Bill actually seemed to understand and believe it. But then, he'd known Dad a lot better than I did.

"I've remarked before on the resemblance you bear your father."

I nodded.

"It goes beyond the physical," he continued. "For a while there he had a habit of showing up like a downed fighter pilot behind enemy lines. I'll never forget the night he arrived on horseback with a sword at his side and had me trace a missing compost heap for him." He chuckled. "Now you come along with a story that makes me believe Pandora's box has been opened again. Why couldn't you just want a divorce like any sensible young man? Or a will written or a trust set up? A partnership agreement? Something like that? No, this sounds more like one of Carl's problems. Even the other stuff I've done for Amber seems pretty sedate by comparison."

"Other stuff? You mean the Concord—the time Random sent Fiona with a copy of the Patternfall Treaty with Swayvil, King of Chaos, for her to translate and you to look at for loopholes?"

"That, yes," he said, "though I wound up studying your language myself before I was done. Then Flora wanted her library recovered—no easy job—and then an old flame traced—whether for reunion or revenge I never learned. Paid me in gold, though. Bought the place in Palm Beach with it. Then—Oh, hell. For a while there, I thought of adding 'Counsel to the Court of Amber' to my business card. But that sort of work was understandable. I do similar things on a mundane level all the time. Yours, though, has that black magic and sudden-death quality to it that seemed to follow your father about. It scares the hell out of me, and I wouldn't even know how to go about advising you on it."

"Well, the black magic and sudden-death parts are my area, I guess," I observed. "In fact, they may color my thinking too much. You're bound to look at things a lot differently than I do. A blind spot by definition is something you're not aware of. What might I be missing?"

He took a sip of his beer, lit his pipe again.

"Okay," he said. "Your friend Luke—where's he from?"

"Somewhere in the Midwest, I believe he said: Nebraska, Iowa, Ohio—one of those places."

"Mm-hm. What line of work is his old man in?"

"He never mentioned it."

"Does he have any brothers or sisters?"

"I don't know. He never said."

"Doesn't that strike you as somewhat odd—that he never mentioned his family or talked about his home town in the whole eight years you've known him?"

"No. After all, I never talked about mine either."

"It's not natural, Merle. You grew up in a strange place that you *couldn't* talk about. You had every reason to change the subject, avoid the issues. He obviously did, too. And then, back when you came you weren't even certain how most people here behaved. But didn't you ever wonder about Luke?"

"Of course. But he respected my reticence. I could do

no less for him. You might say that we had a sort of tacit agreement that such things were off limits."

"How'd you meet him?"

"We were freshmen together, had a lot of the same classes."

"And you were both strangers in town, no other friends. You hit it off from the beginning..."

"No. We barely talked to each other. I thought he was an arrogant bastard who felt he was ten times better than anybody he'd ever met. I didn't like him, and he didn't like me much either."

"Why not?"

"He felt the same way about me."

"So it was only gradually that you came to realize you were both wrong?"

"No. We were both right. We got to know each other by trying to show each other up. If I'd do something kind of— outstanding—he'd try to top it. And vice versa. We got so we'd go out for the same sport, try to date the same girls, try to beat each other's grades."

"And...?"

"Somewhere along the line I guess we started to respect each other. When we both made the Olympic finals something broke. We started slapping each other on the back and laughing, and we went out and had dinner and sat up all night talking and he said he didn't give a shit about the Olympics and I said I didn't either. He said he'd just wanted to show me he was a better man and now he didn't care anymore. He'd decided we were both good enough, and he'd just as soon let the matter stand at that. I felt exactly the same way and told him so. That was when we got to be friends."

"I can understand that," Bill said. "It's a specialized sort of friendship. You're friends in certain places."

I laughed and took a drink.

"Isn't everyone?"

"At first, yes. Sometimes always. Nothing wrong with

that. It's just that yours seems a much more highly specialized friendship than most."

I nodded slowly. "Maybe so."

"So it still doesn't make sense. Two guys as close as you got to be—with no pasts to show to each other."

"I guess you're right. What does it mean?"

"You're not a normal human being."

"No, I'm not."

"I'm not so sure Luke is either."

"What, then?"

"That's your department."

I nodded.

"Apart from that issue," Bill continued, "something else has been bothering me."

"What?"

"This Martinez fellow. He followed you out to the boondocks, stopped when you did, stalked you, then opened fire. Who was he after? Both of you? Just Luke? Or just you?"

"I don't know. I'm not sure which of us that first shot was aimed for. After that, he was firing at Luke—because by then Luke was attacking and he was defending himself."

"Exactly. If he were S—or S's agent—why would he even have bothered with that conversation with you in the bar?"

"I now have the impression that the whole thing was an elaborate buildup to that final question of his, as to whether Luke knew anything about Amber."

"And your reaction, rather than your answer, led him to believe that he did."

"Well, apparently Luke does—from the way he addressed me right there at the end. You think he was really gunning for someone from Amber?"

"Maybe. Luke is no Amberite, though?"

"I never heard of anyone like him in the time I spent there after the war. And I got plenty of lectures on genealogy. My relatives are like a sewing circle when it comes to keeping track of such matters—a lot less orderly about it than they are in Chaos—can't even decide exactly who's oldest, because some of them were born in different time streams—but they're pretty thorough—"

"Chaos! That's right! You're also lousy with relatives on that side! Could—?"

I shook my head. "No way. I have an even more extensive knowledge of the families there. I believe I'm acquainted with just about all of the ones who can manipulate Shadow, traverse it. Luke's not one of them and—"

"Wait a minute! There are people in the Courts who can walk in Shadow, also?"

"Yes. Or stay in one place and bring things from Shadow to them. It's a kind of reverse—"

"I thought you had to walk the Pattern to gain that power?"

"They have a sort of equivalent called the Logrus. It's a kind of chaotic maze. Keeps shifting about. Very dangerous. Unbalances you mentally, too, for a time. No fun."

"So you've done it?"

"Yes."

"And you walked the Pattern as well?"

I licked my lips, remembering.

"Yes. Damn near killed me. Suhuy'd thought it would, but Fiona thought I could make it if she helped. I was—"

"Who's Suhuy?"

"He's Master of the Logrus. He's an uncle of mine, too. He felt that the Pattern of Amber and the Logrus of Chaos were incompatible, that I could not bear the images of both within me. Random, Fiona, and Gérard had taken me down to show me the Pattern. I got in touch with Suhuy then and gave him a look at it. He said that they seemed antithetical, and that I would either be destroyed by the attempt or the Pattern would drive the image of the Logrus from me— probably the former. But Fiona said that the Pattern should be able to encompass anything, even the Logrus, and from what she understood of the Logrus it should be able to work its way around anything, even the Pattern. So they left it up to me, and I knew that I had to walk it. So I did. I made it, and I still bear the Logrus as well as the Pattern. Suhuy acknowledged that Fi had been right, and he speculated that it had to do with my mixed parentage. She disagreed, though—"

Bill raised his hand. "Wait a minute. I don't understand how you got your uncle Suhuy down into the basement of Amber Castle on a moment's notice."

"Oh, I have a set of Chaos Trumps as well as a set of Amber Trumps, for my relatives back in the Courts."

He shook his head. "All of this is fascinating, but we're straying from the point. Is there anyone else who can walk in Shadow? Or are there other ways of doing it?"

"Yes, there are different ways it could be done. There are a number of magical beings, like the Unicorn, who can just wander wherever they want. And you can follow a Shadow walker or a magical being through Shadow for for so long as you can keep track of it, no matter who you are. Kind of like Thomas Rhymer is the ballad. And one Shadow walker could lead an army through. And then there are the inhabitants of the various Shadow kingdoms nearest to Amber and to Chaos. Those at both ends breed mighty sorcerers, just because of their proximity to the two power centers. Some of the good ones can become fairly adept at it—but their images of the Pattern or the Logrus are imperfect, so they're never quite as good as the real thing. But on either end they don't even need an initiation to wander on in. The Shadow interfaces are thinnest there. We even have commerce with them, actually. And established routes become easier and easier to follow with time. Going outward is harder, though. But large attacking forces have been known to come through. That's why we maintain patrols. Julian in Arden, Gérard at sea, and so forth."

"Any other ways?"

"A Shadow-storm perhaps."

"What's that?"

"It's a natural but not too well-understood phenomenon. The best comparison I can think of is a tropical storm. One theory as to their origin has to do with the beat frequencies of waves that pulse outward from Amber and from the Courts, shaping the nature of shadows. Whatever, when such a storm rises it can flow through a large number of shadows before it plays itself out. Sometimes they do a lot of damage, sometimes very little. But they often transport things in their progress."

"Does that include people?"

"It's been known to happen."

He finished his beer. I did the same with mine.

"What about the Trumps?" he asked. "Could anybody learn to use them?"

"Yes."

"How many sets are there kicking around?"

"I don't know."

"Who makes them?"

"There are a number of experts in the Courts. That's where I learned. And there are Fiona and Bleys back in Amber—and I believe they were teaching Random—"

"Those sorcerers you spoke of—from the adjacent kingdoms . . . Could any of them do up a set of Trumps?"

"Yes, but theirs would be less than perfect. It is my understanding that you have to be an initiate of either the Pattern or the Logrus to do them properly. Some of them could do a sort of half-assed set, though, one you'd be taking your chances on using—maybe winding up dead or in some limbo, sometimes getting where you were headed."

"And the set you found at Julia's place . . . ?"

"They're the real thing."

"How do you account for them?"

"Someone who knew how to do it taught someone else who was able to learn it, and I never heard about it. That's all."

"I see."

"I'm afraid none of this is too productive."

"But I need it all to think with," he replied. "How else can I come up with lines of inquiry? You ready for another beer?"

"Wait."

I closed my eyes and visualized an image of the Logrus—shifting, ever shifting. I framed my desire and two of the

swimming lines within the eidolon increased in brightness
and thickness. I moved my arms slowly, imitating their
undulations, their jerkings. Finally, the lines and my arms
seemed to be one, and I opened my hands and extended the
lines outward, outward through Shadow.

Bill cleared his throat.

"Uh—what are you doing, Merle?"

"Looking for something," I replied. "Just a minute."

The lines would keep extending through an infinitude of
Shadow till they encountered the objects of my desire—or
until I ran out of patience or concentration. Finally, I felt
the jerks, like bites on a pair of fishing lines.

"There they are," I said, and I reeled them in quickly.

An icy bottle of beer appeared in each of my hands. I
grasped them as they did and passed one to Bill.

"That's what I meant by the reverse of a Shadow walk,"
I said, breathing deeply a few times. "I sent out to Shadow
for a couple of beers. Saved you a trip to the kitchen."

He regarded the orange label with the peculiar green
script on it.

"I don't recognize the brand," he said, "let alone the
language. You sure it's safe?"

"Yes, I ordered real beer."

"Uh—you didn't happen to pick up an opener, too, did
you?"

"Oops!" I said. "Sorry. I'll—"

"That's all right."

He got up, walked out to the kitchen, and came back a
little later with an opener. When he opened the first one it
foamed a bit and he had to hold it over the wastebasket till
it settled. The same with the other.

"Things can get a bit agitated when you pull them in fast
the way I did," I explained. "I don't usually get my beer
that way and I forgot—"

"That's okay," Bill said, wiping his hands on his handkerchief . . .

He tasted his beer then.

"At least it's good beer," he observed. "I wonder . . . Naw."

"What?"

"Could you send out for a pizza?"

"What do you want on it?" I asked.

The next morning we took a long walk beside a wandering creek, which we met at the back of some farmland owned by a neighbor and client of his. We strolled slowly, Bill with a stick in his hand and a pipe in his mouth, and he continued the previous evening's questioning.

"Something you said didn't really register properly at the time," he stated, "because I was more interested in other aspects of the situation. You say that you and Luke actually made it up to the finals for the Olympics and then dropped out?"

"Yes."

"What area?"

"Several different track and field events. We were both runners and—"

"And his time was close to yours?"

"Damn close. And sometimes it was mine that was close to his."

"Strange."

"What?"

The bank grew steeper, and we crossed on some stepping-stones to the other side where the way was several feet wider and relatively flat, with a well-trod path along it.

"It strikes me as more than a little coincidental," he said, "that this guy should be about as good as you are in sports. From all I've heard, you Amberites are several times stronger than a normal human being, with a fancy metabolism giving you unusual stamina and recuperative and regenerative powers. How come Luke should be able to match you in high-level performances?"

"He's a fine athlete and he keeps himself in good shape," I answered. "There are other people like that here—very strong and fast."

He shook his head as we started out along the path.

"I'm not arguing that," he said. "It's just that it seems like one coincidence too many. This guy hides his past the same way you do, and then it turns that he really knows who you are anyhow. Tell me, is he really a big art buff?"

"Huh?"

"Art. He really cared enough about art to collect it?"

"Oh. Yes. We used to hit gallery openings and museum exhibits fairly regularly."

He snorted and swung his stick at a pebble, which splashed into the stream.

"Well," he observed, "that weakens one point, but hardly destroys the pattern."

"I don't follow..."

"It seemed odd that he also knew that crazy occultist painter. Less odd, though, when you say that the guy was good and that Luke really did collect art."

"He didn't have to tell me that he knew Melman."

"True. But all of this plus his physical abilities... I'm just building a circumstantial case, or course, but I feel that guy is very unusual."

I nodded.

"I've been over it in my mind quite a few times since last night," I said. "If he's not really from here, I don't know where the hell he's from."

"Then we may have exhausted this line of inquiry," Bill said, leading me around a bend and pausing to watch some birds take flight from a marshy area across the water. He glanced back in the direction from which we had come, then, "Tell me—completely off the subject—what's your—uh, rank?" he asked.

"What do you mean?"

"You're the son of a Prince of Amber. What does that make you?"

"You mean titles? I'm Duke of the Western Marches and Earl of Kolvir."

"What does that mean?"

"It means I'm not a Prince of Amber. Nobody has to

worry about me scheming, no vendettas involving the succession—"

"Hm."

"What do you mean, 'Hm'?"

He shrugged. "I've read too much history. Nobody's safe."

I shrugged myself. "Last I heard, everything was peaceful on the home front."

"Well, that's good news, anyway."

A few more turnings brought us to a wide area of pebbles and sand, rising gently for perhaps thirty feet to the place where it met an abrupt embankment seven or eight feet in height. I could see the high water line and a number of exposed roots from trees that grew along the top. Bill seated himself on a boulder back in their shade and relit his pipe. I rested on one nearby, to his left. The water splashed and rippled in a comfortable key, and we watched it sparkle for a time.

"Nice," I said, a bit later. "Pretty place."

"Uh-huh."

I glanced at him. Bill was looking back the way we'd come.

I lowered my voice. "Something there?"

"I caught a glimpse a little earlier," he whispered, "of someone else taking a walk this way—some distance behind us. Lost sight of him in all the turnings we took."

"Maybe I should take a stroll back."

"Probably nothing. It's a beautiful day. A lot of people do like to hike around here. Just thought that if we waited a few minutes he'd either show up or we'd know he'd gone somewhere else."

"Can you describe him?"

"Nope. Caught only the barest glimpse. I don't think it's anything to get excited about. It's just that thinking about your story made me a little wary—or paranoid. I'm not sure which."

I found my own pipe and packed it and lit it and we

waited. For fifteen minutes or so we waited. But no one showed.

Finally, Bill rose and stretched. "False alarm," he said. "I guess."

He started walking again and I fell in step beside him.

"Then that Jasra lady bothers me," he said. "You say she seemed to trump in—and then she had that sting in her mouth that knocked you for a loop?"

"Right."

"Ever encounter anyone like her before?"

"No."

"Any guesses?"

I shook my head.

"And why the Walpurgisnacht business? I can see a certain date having significance for a psycho, and I can see people in various primitive religions placing great importance on the turning of the seasons. But S seems almost too well organized to be a mental case. And as for the other—"

"Melman thought it was important."

"Yes, but he was into that stuff. I'd be surprised if he didn't come up with such a correspondence, whether it was intended or not. He admitted that his master had never told him that that was the case. It was his own idea. But you're the one with the background in the area. Is there any special significance or any real power that you know of to be gained by slaying someone of your blood at this particular time of year?"

"None that I ever heard of. But of course there are a lot of things I don't know about. I'm very young compared to most of the adepts. But which way are you trying to go on this? You say you don't think it's a nut, but you don't buy the Walpurgis notion either."

"I don't know. I'm just thinking out loud. They both sound shaky to me; that's all. For that matter, the French Foreign Legion gave everyone leave on April 30 to get drunk, and a couple of days after that to sober up. It's the anniversary of the battle of Camerone, one of their big triumphs. But I doubt that figures in this either.

"And why the sphinx?" he said suddenly. "Why a Trump that takes you someplace to trade dumb riddles or get your head bitten off?"

"I'd a feeling it was more the latter that was intended."

"I sort of think so, too. But it's certainly bizarre. You know what? I'll bet they're all that way—traps of some kind."

"Could be."

I put my hand in my pocket, reaching for them.

"Leave them," he said. "Let's not look for trouble. Maybe you should ditch them, at least for a while. I could put them in my safe, down at the office."

I laughed.

"Safes aren't all that safe. No thanks. I want them with me. There may be a way of checking them out without any risk."

"You're the expert. But tell me, could something sneak through from the scene on the card without you—"

"No. They don't work that way. They require your attention to operate. More than a little of it."

"That's something, anyway. I—"

He looked back again. Someone was coming. I flexed my fingers, involuntarily.

Then I heard him let go a big breath.

"It's okay," he said. "I know him. It's George Hansen. He's the son of the guy who owns the farm we're behind. Hi, George!"

The approaching figure waved. He was of medium height and stocky build. Had sandy hair. He wore Levi's and a Grateful Dead T-shirt, a pack of cigarettes twisted into its left sleeve. He looked to be in his twenties.

"Hi," he answered, drawing near. "Swell day, huh?"

"Sure is," Bill answered. "That's why we're out walking in it, instead of sitting at home."

George's gaze shifted to me.

"Me, too," he said, raking his teeth over his lower lip. "Real good day."

"This is Merle Corey. He's visiting me."

"Merle Corey," George repeated, and he stuck out his hand. "Hi, Merle."

I took it and shook it. It was a little clammy.

"Recognize the name?"

"Uh—Merle Corey," he said again.

"You knew his dad."

"Yeah? Oh, sure!"

"Sam Corey," Bill finished, and he shot me a glance over George's shoulder.

"Sam Corey," George repeated. "Son of a gun! Good to know you. You going to be here long?"

"A few days, I guess," I replied. "I didn't realize you'd known my father."

"Fine man," he said. "Where you from?"

"California, but it's time for a change."

"Where you headed?"

"Out of the country, actually."

"Europe?"

"Farther."

"Sounds great. I'd like to travel sometime."

"Maybe you will."

"Maybe. Well, I'll be moving on. Let you guys enjoy your walk. Nice meeting you, Merle."

"My pleasure."

He backed away, waved, turned, and walked off.

I glanced at Bill then and noticed that he was shaking.

"What's the matter?" I whispered.

"I've known that boy all his life," he said. "Do you think he's on drugs?"

"Not the kind you have to make holes in your arms for. I didn't see any tracks. And he didn't seem particularly spacey."

"Yeah, but you don't know him the way I do. He seemed very—different. It was just on impulse that I used the name Sam for your dad, because something didn't seem right.

His speech patterns have changed, his posture, his gait . . . Intangibles. I was waiting for him to correct me, and then I could have made a joke about premature senility. But he didn't. He picked up on it instead. Merle, this is scary! He knew your father real well—as Carl Corey. Your dad liked to keep his place nice, but he was never much for weeding and mowing or raking leaves. George did his yard work for him for years while he was in school. He knew his name wasn't Sam."

"I don't understand."

"Neither do I," he said, "and I don't like it."

"So he's acting weird—and you think he was following us?"

"Now I do. This is too much of a coincidence, timed with your arrival."

I turned.

"I'm going after him," I said. "I'll find out."

"No. Don't."

"I won't hurt him. There are other ways."

"It might be better to let him think he's got us fooled. It might encourage him to do something or say something later that could prove useful. On the other hand, anything you do—even something subtle or magical—might let him, or something, know that we're on to him. Let it ride, be grateful you're warned and be wary."

"You've got a point there," I agreed. "Okay."

"Let's head on back and drive into town for lunch. I want to stop by the office and pick up some papers and make some phone calls. Then I have to see a client at two o'clock. You can take the car and knock around while I'm doing that."

"Fine."

As we strolled back I did some wondering. There were a number of things I had not told Bill. For instance, there had been no reason to tell him that I wore an invisible strangling cord possessed of some rather unusual virtues, woven about my left wrist. One of these virtues is that it generally warns me of nasty intentions aimed in my direction, as it had done in Luke's presence for almost two years until we became friends. Whatever the reason for George Hansen's unusual behavior, Frakir had not given me any indication that he meant me harm.

Funny, though . . . there was something about the way he talked, the way he said his words . . .

I went for a drive after lunch while Bill took care of his business. I headed out to the place where my father had lived years ago. I'd been by it a number of times in the past, but I'd never been inside. No real reason to, I guess, anyway. I parked up the road on a rise, off on the shoulder, and regarded it. A young couple lived there now, Bill had told me, with some kids—a thing I could see for myself from some scattered toys off to the side of the yard. I wondered what it would have been like, growing up in a place like that. I supposed that I could have. The house looked well kept, sprightly even. I imagined that the people were happy there.

I wondered where he was—if he were even among the living. No one could reach him via his Trump, though that didn't necessarily prove anything. There are a variety of ways in which a Trump sending can be blocked. In fact one of these situations was even said to apply in his case, though I didn't like to think about it.

One rumor had it that Dad had been driven mad in the Courts of Chaos by a curse placed upon him by my mother, and that he now wandered aimlessly through Shadow. She refused even to comment on this story. Another was that he had entered the universe of his own creation and never returned, which it seemed possible could remove him from the reach of the Trumps. Another was simply that he had perished at some point after his departure from the Courts— and a number of my relatives there assured me that they had seen him leave after his sojourn. So, if the rumor of his death were correct, it did not occur in the Courts of Chaos. And there were others who claimed to have seen him at widely separated sites afterward, encounters invariably involving bizarre behavior on his part. I had been told by one that he was traveling in the company of a mute dancer—a tiny, lovely lady with whom he communicated by means of sign language—and that he wasn't talking much himself either. Another reported him as roaring drunk in a raucous cantina, from which he eventually expelled all the other patrons in order to enjoy the music of the band without distraction. I could not vouch for the authenticity of any of these accounts. It had taken me a lot of searching just to come up with this handful of rumors. I could not locate him with a Logrus summoning either, though I had tried many times. But of course if he were far enough afield my powers of concentration may simply have been inadequate.

In other words, I didn't know where the hell my father, Corwin of Amber, was, and nobody else seemed to know either. I regretted this sorely, because my only long encounter with him had been on the occasion of hearing his lengthy story outside the Courts of Chaos on the day of the Patternfall battle. This had changed my life. It had given me the resolve to depart the Court, with the determination to seek experience and education in the shadow world where he had dwelled for so long. I'd felt a need to understand it if I were to understand him better. I believed that I had now achieved something of this, and more. But he was no longer available to continue our conversation.

I believed that I was about ready to attempt a new means of locating him—now that the Ghostwheel project was almost off the ground—when the most recent fecal missile met the rotating blades. Following my cross-country trip, scheduled to wind up at Bill's place a month or two from now, I was going to head off to my personal anomaly of a place and begin the work.

Now . . . other things had crowded in. The matters at hand would have to be dealt with before I could get on with the search.

I drove past the house slowly. I could hear the sounds of stereo music through open windows. Better not to know exactly what it was like inside. Sometimes a little mystery is best.

That evening after dinner I sat on the porch with Bill, trying to think of anything else I should run through his mind. As I kept drawing blanks, he was the first to renew our serial conversation:

"Something else," he began.

"Yes?"

"Dan Martinez struck up his conversation with you by alluding to Luke's attempts to locate investors for some sort of computer company. You later felt that the whole thing could simply have been a ploy, to get you off guard and then hit you with that question about Amber and Chaos."

"Right."

"But then Luke really did raise the matter of doing something along those lines. He insisted, though, that he had not been in touch with potential investors and that he had never heard of Dan Martinez. When he saw the man dead later he still maintained that he'd never met him."

I nodded.

"Then either Luke was lying, or Martinez had somehow learned his plans."

"I don't think Luke was lying," I said. "In fact, I've been thinking about that whole business some more. Just knowing him as I do, I don't believe Luke *would* have gone around looking for investors until he was sure there was something to put the money into. I think he was telling the truth on that, too. It seems more likely to me that this might have been the only real coincidence in everything that's happened so far. I have the feeling that Martinez knew a lot about Luke and just wanted that one final piece of information—about his knowledge of Amber and the Courts. I think he was very shrewd, and on the basis of what he knew already he was able to concoct something that seemed plausible to me, knowing I'd worked for the same company as Luke."

"I suppose it's possible," he said. "But then when Luke really did—"

"I'm beginning to believe," I interrupted, "that Luke's story was phoney, too."

"I don't follow you."

"I think he put it together the same way Martinez did, and for similar reasons—to sound plausible to me so that he could get some information he wanted."

"You've lost me. What information?"

"My Ghostwheel. He wanted to know what it was."

"And he was disappointed to learn that it was just an exercise in exotic design, for other reasons than building a company?"

Bill caught my smile as I nodded.

"There's more?" he said. Then: "Wait. Don't tell me. You were lying, too. It's something real."

"Yes."

"I probably shouldn't even ask—unless you think it's material and want to tell me. If it's something big and very important it could be gotten out of me, you know. I have a low tolerance for pain. Think about it."

I did. I sat there for some time, musing.

"I suppose it could be," I said finally, "in a sort of peripheral way I'm sure you're not referring to. But I don't see how it could be—as you say—material. Not to Luke or to anyone else—because nobody even knows what it is but me. No. I can't see how it enters the equation beyond Luke's curiosity about it. So I think I'll follow your suggestion and just keep it off the record."

"Fine with me," he said. "Then there is the matter of Luke's disappearance—"

Within the house, a telephone rang.

"Excuse me," Bill said.

He rose and went into the kitchen.

After a few moments, I heard him call, "Merle, it's for you!"

I got up and went inside. I gave him a questioning look as soon as I entered and he shrugged and shook his head. I thought fast and recalled the location of two other phones in the house. I pointed at him, pointed in the direction of his study and pantomimed the motion of picking up a receiver and holding it to one's ear. He smiled slightly and nodded.

I took the receiver and waited a while, till I heard the click, only beginning to speak then, hoping the caller would think I'd picked up an extension to answer.

"Hello," I said.

"Merle Corey?"

"That's me."

"I need some information I think you might have."

It was a masculine voice, sort of familiar but not quite.

"Who am I talking to?" I asked.

"I'm sorry. I can't tell you that."

"Then that will probably be my answer to your question, too."

"Will you at least let me ask?"

"Go ahead," I said.

"Okay. You and Luke Raynard are friends."

He paused.

"You could say that," I said, to fill the space.

"You have heard him speak of places called Amber and the Courts of Chaos."

Again, a statement rather than a question.

"Maybe," I said.

"Do you know anything of these places yourself?"

Finally, a question.

"Maybe," I said again.

"Please. This is serious. I need something more than a 'maybe.'"

"Sorry. 'Maybe' is all you're going to get, unless you tell me who you are and why you want to know."

"I can be of great service to you if you will be honest with me."

I bit back a reply just in time and felt my pulse begin to race. That last statement had been spoken in Thari. I maintained my silence.

Then: "Well, that didn't work, and I still don't really know."

"What? What don't you know?" I said.

"Whether he's from one of those places or whether it's you."

"To be as blunt as possible, what's it to you?" I asked him.

"Because one of you may be in great danger."

"The one who is from such a place or the one who is not?" I asked.

"I can't tell you that. I can't afford another mistake."

"What do you mean? What was your last one about?"

"You won't tell me—either for purposes of self-preservation, or to help a friend?"

"I might," I said, "if I knew that that were really the case. But for all I know, it might be you that's the danger."

"I assure you I am only trying to help the right person."

"Words, words, words," I said. "Supposing we were both from such places?"

"Oh, my!" he said. "No. That couldn't be."

"Why not?"

"Never mind. What do I have to do to persuade you?"

"Mm. Wait a minute. Let me think," I answered. "All right. How about this? I'll meet you someplace. You name the place. I get a good look at you and we trade information, one piece at a time, till all the cards are on the table."

There was a pause.

Then: "That's the only way you'll do it?"

"Yes."

"Let me think about it. I'll be back in touch soon."

"One thing—"

"What?"

"If it is me, am I in danger right now?"

"I think so. Yes, you probably are. Good-bye."

He hung up.

I managed to sigh and swear at the same time as I recradled the phone. People who knew about us seemed to be coming out of the woodwork.

Bill came into the kitchen, a very puzzled expression on his face.

"How'd whoever-the-hell-he-is even know you're here?" were his first words.

"That was my question," I said. "Think up another."

"I will. If he wants to set something up, are you really going?"

"You bet. I suggested it because I want to meet this guy."

"As you pointed out, he may be the danger."

"That's okay by me. He's going to be in a lot of danger, too."

"I don't like it."

"I'm not so happy with it myself. But it's the best offer I've had so far."

"Well, it's your decision. It's too bad there isn't some way of locating him beforehand."

"That passed through my mind, too."

"Listen, why not push him a little?"

"How?"

"He sounded a little nervous, and I don't think he liked your suggestion any more than I do. Let's not be here when he calls back. Don't let him think you're just sitting around waiting for the phone to ring. Make him wait a little. Go conjure up some fresh clothes and we'll drive over to the country club for a couple of hours. It'll beat raiding the icebox."

"Good idea," I said. "This was supposed to be a vacation, one time. That's probably the closest I'll get. Sounds fine."

I renewed my wardrobe out of Shadow, trimmed my beard, showered, and dressed. We drove to the club then and had a leisurely meal on the terrace. It was a good evening for it, balmy and star-filled, running with moonlight like milk. By mutual consent we refrained from discussing my problems any further. Bill seemed to know almost everyone there, so it seemed a friendly place to me. It was the most relaxed evening I'd spent in a long while. Afterward we stopped for drinks in the club bar, which I gathered had been one of my dad's favorite watering spots, strains of dance music drifting through from the room next door.

"Yeah, it was a good idea," I said. "Thanks."

"De nada," he said. "I had a lot of good times here with your old man. You haven't, by any chance—?"

"No, no news of him."

"Sorry."

"I'll let you know when he turns up."

"Sure. Sorry."

The drive back was uneventful, and no one followed us. We got in a little after midnight, said good night, and I went straight to my room. I shrugged out of my new jacket and hung it in the closet, kicked off my new shoes and left them there, too. As I walked back into the room, I noticed the white rectangle on the pillow of my bed.

I crossed to it in two big steps and snatched it up.

SORRY YOU WERE NOT IN WHEN I CALLED BACK, it said, in block capitals. BUT I SAW YOU AT THE CLUB AND CAN CERTAINLY UNDERSTAND YOUR WANTING A NIGHT OUT. IT GAVE ME AN IDEA. LET'S MEET IN THE BAR THERE, TOMORROW NIGHT, AT TEN. I'D FEEL BETTER WITH LOTS OF PEOPLE AROUND BUT NONE OF THEM LISTENING.

Damn. My first impulse was to go and tell Bill. My first thought following the impulse, though, was that there was nothing he could do except lose some sleep over it, a thing he probably needed a lot more than I did. So I folded the note and stuck it in my shirt pocket, then hung up the shirt.

Not even a nightmare to liven my slumber. I slept deeply and well, knowing Frakir would rouse me in the event of danger. In fact, I overslept, and it felt good. The morning was sunny and birds were singing.

I made my way downstairs to the kitchen after splashing and combing myself into shape and raiding Shadow for fresh slacks and a shirt. There was a note on the kitchen table. I was tired of finding notes, but this one was from Bill, saying he'd had to run into town to his office for a while and I should go ahead and help myself to anything that looked good for breakfast. He'd be back a little later.

I checked out the refrigerator and came up with some

English muffins, a piece of cantaloupe and a glass of orange juice. Some coffee I'd started first thing was ready shortly after I finished, and I took a cup with me out onto the porch.

As I sat there, I began to think that maybe I ought to leave a note of my own and move on. My mysterious correspondent—conceivably S—had phoned here once and broken in once. How S had known I was here was immaterial. It was a friend's house, and though I did not mind sharing some of my problems with friends, I did not like the idea of exposing them to danger. But then, it was daylight now and the meeting was set for this evening. Not that much longer till some sort of resolution was achieved. Almost silly to depart at this point. In fact, it was probably better that I hang around till then. I could keep an eye on things, protect Bill if anything came up today—

Suddenly, I had a vision of someone forcing Bill to write that note at gunpoint, then whisking him away as a hostage to pressure me into answering questions.

I hurried back to the kitchen and phoned his office. Horace Crayper, his secretary, answered on the second ring.

"Hi, this is Merle Corey," I said. "Is Mr. Roth in?"

"Yes," he replied, "but he's with a client right now. Could I have him call you back?"

"No, it's not that important," I said, "and I'll be seeing him later. Don't bother him. Thanks."

I poured myself another cup of coffee and returned to the porch. This sort of thing was bad for the nerves. I decided that if everything wasn't squared away this evening I would leave.

A figure rounded the corner of the house.

"Hi, Merle."

It was George Hansen. Frakir gave me the tiniest of pulses, as if beginning a warning and then reconsidering it. Ambiguous. Unusual.

"Hi, George. How's it going?"

"Pretty well. Is Mr. Roth in?"

"Afraid not. He had to go into town for a while. I imagine he'll be back around lunchtime or a little after."

"Oh. A few days ago he'd asked me to stop by when I was free, about some work he wanted done."

He came nearer, put his foot on the step.

I shook my head.

"Can't help you. He didn't mention it to me. You'll have to catch him later."

He nodded, unwound his pack of cigarettes, shook one out and lit it, then rewound the pack in his shirt sleeves. This T-shirt was a Pink Floyd.

"How are you enjoying your stay?" he asked.

"Real well. You care for a cup of coffee?"

"Don't mind if I do."

I rose and went inside.

"With a little cream and sugar," he called after me.

I fixed him one and when I returned with it he was seated in the other chair on the porch.

"Thanks."

After he'd tasted it, he said, "I know your dad's name's Carl even though Mr. Roth said Sam. His memory must've slipped."

"Or his tongue," I said.

He smiled.

What was it about the way he talked? His voice could almost be the one I'd heard on the phone last night, though that one had been very controlled and slowed just enough to neutralize any number of speech clues. It wasn't that comparison that was bothering me.

"He was a retired military officer, wasn't he? And some sort of government consultant?"

"Yes."

"Where is he now?"

"Doing a lot of traveling—overseas."

"You going to see him on your own trip?"

"I hope so."

"That'll be nice," he said, taking a drag on his cigarette and another sip of coffee. "Ah! that's good!"

"I don't remember seeing you around," he said suddenly then. "You never lived with your dad, huh?"

"No, I grew up with my mother and other relatives."

"Pretty far from here, huh?"

I nodded. "Overseas."

"What was her name?"

I almost told him. I'm not certain why. But I changed it to "Dorothy" before it came out.

I glanced at him in time to see him purse his lips. He had been studying my face as I spoke.

"Why do you ask?" I said.

"No special reason. Or genetic nosiness, you might say. *My* mother was the town gossip."

He laughed and gulped coffee.

"Will you be staying long?" he asked then.

"Hard to say. Probably not real long, though."

"Well, I hope you have a good time of it." He finished his coffee and set the cup on the railing. He rose then, stretched and added, "Nice talking to you."

Partway down the stairs he paused and turned.

"I've a feeling you'll go far," he told me. "Good luck."

"You may, too," I said. "You've a way with words."

"Thanks for the coffee. See you around."

"Yes."

He turned the corner and was gone. I simply didn't know what to make of him, and after several attempts I gave up. When inspiration is silent reason tires quickly.

I was making myself a sandwich when Bill returned, so I made two. He went and changed clothes while I was doing this.

"I'm supposedly taking it easy this month," he said while we were eating, "but that was an old client with some pressing business, so I had to go in. What say we follow the creek in the other direction this afternoon?"

"Sure."

As we hiked across the field I told him of George's visit.

"No," he said, "I didn't tell him I had any jobs for him."

"In other words—"

"I guess he came by to see you. It would have been easy enough to see me leave, from their place."

"I wish I knew what he wanted."

"If it's important enough he'll probably wind up asking you, in time."

"But time is running," I said. "I've decided to leave tomorrow morning, maybe even tonight."

"Why?"

As we made our way down the creek, I told him of last night's note and this evening's rendezvous. I also told him my feelings about exposing him to stray shots, or intended ones.

"It may not be that serious," he began.

"My mind's made up, Bill. I hate to cut things short when I haven't seen you for so long, but I hadn't counted on all this trouble. And if I go away you know that it will, too."

"Probably so, but . . ."

We continued in this vein for a while as we followed the watercourse. Then we finally dropped the matter as settled and returned to a fruitless rehashing of my puzzles. As we walked I looked back occasionally but did not see anyone behind us. I did hear a few sounds within the brush on the opposite bank at infrequent intervals, but it could easily have been an animal disturbed by our voices.

We had hiked for over an hour when I had the premonitory feeling that someone was picking up my Trump. I froze.

Bill halted and turned toward me.

"What—"

I raised my hand.

"Long distance call," I said.

A moment later I felt the first movement of contact. I also heard the noise in the bushes again, across the water.

"Merlin."

It was Random's voice, calling to me. A few seconds later I saw him, seated at a desk in the library of Amber.

"Yes?" I answered.

The image came into solidity, assumed full reality, as if I were looking through an archway into an adjacent room. At the same time, I still possessed my vision of the rest of my surroundings, though it was growing more and more peripheral by the moment. For example, I saw George Hansen start up from among the bushes across the creek, staring at me.

"I want you back in Amber right away," Random stated.

George began to move forward, splashing down into the water.

Random raised his hand, extended it.

"Come on through," he said.

By now my outline must have begun shimmering, and I heard George cry out, "Stop! Wait! I have to come with—!"

I reached out and grasped Bill's shoulder.

"I can't leave you with this nut," I said. "Come on!"

With my other hand I clasped Random's.

"Okay," I said, moving forward.

"Stop!" George cried.

"The hell you say," I replied, and we left him to clasp a rainbow.

CHAPTER 7

Random looked startled as the two of us came through into the library. He rose to his feet, which still left him shorter than either of us, and he shifted his attention to Bill.

"Merlin, who's this?" he asked.

"Your attorney, Bill Roth," I said. "You've always dealt with him through agents in the past. I thought you might like to—"

Bill began dropping to one knee, "Your Majesty," on his lips, but Random caught him by the shoulders.

"Cut the crap," he said. "We're not in Court." He clasped his hand, then said, "Call me Random. I've always intended to thank you personally for the work you did on that treaty. Never got around to it, though. Good to meet you."

I'd never seen Bill at a loss for words before, but he just stared, at Random, at the room, out of the window at a distant tower.

Finally, "It's real . . ." I heard him whisper moments later.

"Did I not see someone springing toward you?" Random said to me, running a hand through his unruly brown hair.

"And surely your last words back there were not addressed to me?"

"We were having a little problem," I answered. "That's the real reason I brought Bill along. You see, someone's been trying to kill me, and—"

Random raised his hand. "Spare me the details for the moment. I'll need them all later, but—but let it be later. There is more nastiness than usual afoot at the moment, and yours may well be a part of it. But I've got to breathe a bit."

It was only then that some deepened lines in his naturally youthful face registered and I began to realize that he was under a strain.

"What's the matter?" I asked.

"Caine is dead. Murdered," he replied. "This morning."

"How did it happen?"

"He was off in Shadow Deiga—a distant port with which we have commerce. He was with Gérard, to renegotiate an old trade agreement. He was shot, through the heart. Died instantly."

"Did they catch the bowman?"

"Bowman, hell! It was a rifleman, on a rooftop. And he got away."

"I thought gunpowder didn't work around here."

He made a quick palms-up gesture.

"Deiga may be far enough off in Shadow for it to work. Nobody here can remember ever testing any there. For that matter, though, your father once came up with a compound that worked here."

"True. I'd almost forgotten."

"Anyway, the funeral is tomorrow—"

"Bill! Merlin!"

My aunt Flora—who had turned down Rossetti's offers, one of them being to model for him—had entered the room. Tall, slim and burnished, she hurried forward and kissed Bill on the cheek. I had never seen him blush before. She repeated the act for me, too, but I was less moved, recalling that she had once been my father's warden.

"When did you get in?" Her voice was lovely, too.

"Just now," I said.

She immediately linked arms with both of us and attempted to lead us off.

"We have so much to talk about," she began.

"Flora!" This from Random.

"Yes, brother?"

"You may give Mr. Roth the full tour, but I require Merlin's presence for a time."

She pouted slightly for a moment, then released my arm.

"Now you know what an absolute monarchy is," she explained to Bill. "You can see how power corrupts."

"I was corrupt before I had power," Random said, "and rich is better. You have my leave to depart, sister."

She sniffed and led Bill away.

"It's always quieter around here when she finds a boyfriend off somewhere in Shadow," Random observed. "Unfortunately, she's been home for the better part of a year this time."

I made a tsking sound.

He gestured toward a chair and I took it. He crossed to a cabinet then.

"Wine?" he asked.

"Don't mind if I do."

He poured two glasses, brought me one, and seated himself in a chair to my left, a small table between us.

"Someone also took a shot at Bleys," he said, "this afternoon, in another shadow. Hit him, too, but not bad. Gunman got away. Bleys was just on a diplomatic mission to a friendly kingdom."

"Same person, you think?"

"Sure. We've never had rifle sniping in the neighborhood before. Then two, all of a sudden? It must be the same person. Or the same conspiracy."

"Any clues?"

He shook his head and tasted the wine.

"I wanted to talk to you alone," he said then, "before

any of the others got to you. There are two things I'd like you to know."

I sipped the wine and waited.

"The first is that this really scares me. With the attempt on Bleys it no longer appears to have been simply a personal thing directed at Caine. Somebody seems to have it in for us—or at least some of us. Now you say there's someone after you, too."

"I don't know whether there's any connection—"

"Well, neither do I. But I don't like the possible pattern I see developing. My worst fear is that it may be one or more of us behind it."

"Why?"

He glowered into his goblet.

"For centuries the personal vendetta has been our way of settling disagreements, not necessarily proceeding inevitably to death—though that was always a possibility—but certainly characterized by intrigues, to the end of embarrassing, disadvantaging, maiming, or exiling the other and enhancing one's own position. This reached its latest peak in the scramble for the succession. I thought everything was pretty much settled, though, when I wound up with the job, which I certainly wasn't looking for. I had no real axes to grind, and I've tried to be fair. I know how touchy everyone here is. I don't think it's me, though, and I don't think it's the succession. I haven't had any bad vibes from any of the others. I'd gotten the impression they had decided I was the lesser of all possible evils and were actually cooperating to make it work. No, I don't believe any of the others is rash enough to want my crown. There was actually amity, goodwill, after the succession was settled. But what I'm wondering now is whether the old pattern might be recurring —that some of the others might have taken up the old game again to settle personal grievances. I really don't want to see that happen—all the suspicion, precautions, innuendoes, mistrust, double dealings. It weakens us, and there's always some possible threat or other against which we should be strong. Now, I've spoken with everyone privately, and of course they all deny any knowledge of current cabals, intrigues, and vendettas, but I could see that they're getting suspicious of each other. It's become a habit of thought. And it wasn't at all difficult for them to dig up some old grudge each of the others might still have had against Caine, despite the fact that he saved all our asses by taking out Brand. And the same with Bleys—everyone could find motives for everyone else."

"So you want the killer fast, because of what he's done to morale?"

"Certainly. I don't need all this backbiting and grudge-hunting. It's all still so close to the surface that we're likely to have real cabals, intrigues, and vendettas before long, if we don't already, and some little misunderstanding could lead to violence again."

"*Do* you think it's one of the others?"

"Shit! I'm the same as they are. I get suspicious by reflex. It well may be, but I haven't really seen a bit of evidence."

"Who else could it be?"

He uncrossed and recrossed his legs. He took another drink of wine.

"Hell! Our enemies are legion. But most of them wouldn't have the guts. They all know the kind of reprisal they could expect once we found them out."

He clasped his hands behind his head and stared at the rows of books.

"I don't know how to say this," he began after a time, "but I have to."

I waited again. Then he said quickly, "There's talk it's Corwin, but I don't believe it."

"No," I said softly.

"I told you I don't believe it. Your father means a lot to me."

"Why would anybody believe it?"

"There's a rumor he's gone crazy. You've heard it. What if he's reverted to some past state of mind, from the days when his relations with Caine and Bleys were a lot less than cordial—or with any of us, for that matter? That's what they're saying."

"I don't believe it."

"I just wanted you to be aware that it's being kicked around."

"Nobody'd better kick it in my direction."

He sighed. "Don't *you* start. Please. They're upset. Don't look for trouble."

I took a drink of wine.

"Yes, you're right," I said.

"Now I have to listen to your story. Go ahead, complicate my life some more."

"Okay. At least I'm fresh on it," I told him.

So I ran through it again. It took a long while, and it was getting dark by the time I finished. He had interrupted me only for occasional clarifications and had not indulged in the exploration of contingencies the way Bill had when he'd heard it.

When I had finished, he rose and lit a few oil lamps. I could almost hear him thinking.

Finally he said, "No, you've got me on Luke. He doesn't ring any bells at all. The lady with the sting bothers me a bit, though. It seems I might have heard something about people like that, but I can't recall the circumstances. It'll come to me. I want to know more about this Ghostwheel project of yours, though. Something about it troubles me."

"Sure," I said. "But there is something else I am reminded to tell you first."

"What's that?"

"I covered everything for you pretty much the way I did when I was talking to Bill. In fact, my just having been through it recently made me almost use it like a rehearsal. But there was something I didn't mention to Bill because it didn't seem important at the time. I might even have forgotten it entirely in the light of everything else, till this business about the sniper came up—and then you reminded me that Corwin once developed a substitute for gunpowder that will work here."

"Everybody remembered it, believe me."

"I forgot about two rounds of ammunition I have in my pocket that came from the ruins of that warehouse where Melman had his studio."

"So?"

"They don't contain gunpowder. There's some kind of pink stuff in them instead—and it won't even burn. At least back on that shadow Earth..."

I dug one out.

"Looks like a 30-30," he said.

"I guess so."

Random rose and drew upon a braided cord that hung beside one of the bookshelves.

By the time he'd returned to his seat there was a knock on the door.

"Come in," he called.

A liveried servant entered, a young blond fellow.

"That was quick," Random said.

The man looked puzzled.

"Your Majesty, I do not understand..."

"What's to understand? I rang. You came."

"Sire, I was not on duty in the quarters. I was sent to tell you that dinner is ready to be served, awaiting your pleasure."

"Oh. Tell them I'll be along shortly. As soon as I've spoken with the person I've called."

"Very good, Sire."

The man departed backward with a quick bow.

"I thought that was too good to be true," Random muttered.

A little later another guy appeared, older and less elegantly garbed.

"Rolf, would you run down to the armory and talk to whoever's on duty?" Random said. "Ask him to go through that collection of rifles we have from the time Corwin came to Kolvir with them, the day Eric died. See if he can dig up a 30-30 for me, in good shape. Have him clean it and

send it up. We're going down to dinner now. You can just
leave the weapon in the corner over there."

"30-30, Sire?"

"Right."

Rolf departed, Random rose and stretched. He pocketed
the round I'd given him and gestured toward the door.

"Let's go eat."

"Good idea."

There were eight of us at dinner: Random, Gérard, Flora,
Bill, Martin—who had been called back a little earlier in
the day, Julian—who had just arrived from Arden, Fiona—
who had also just come in, from some distant locale, and
myself. Benedict was due in the morning, and Llewella later
this evening.

I sat to Random's left, Martin to his right. I hadn't seen
Martin in a long while and was curious what he'd been
about. But the atmosphere was not conducive to conversation. As soon as anyone spoke everyone else evinced
unusually acute attention—far beyond the dictates of simple
politeness. I found it rather unnerving, and I guess Random
did, too, because he sent for Droppa MaPantz, the court
jester, to fill the heavy silences.

Droppa had a rough time at first. He began by juggling
some food, eating it as it moved by until it was gone, wiped
his mouth on a borrowed napkin, then insulted each of us
in turn. After that, he commenced a stand-up routine I found
very funny.

Bill, who was at my left, commented softly, "I know
enough Thari to catch most of it, and that's a George Carlin
shtick! How—"

"Oh, whenever Droppa's stuff starts sounding stale, Random sends him off to various clubs in Shadow," I explained,
"to pick up new material. I understand he's a regular at
Vegas. Random even accompanies him sometimes, to play
cards."

He did start getting laughs after a while which loosened
things up a bit. When he knocked off for a drink it became

possible to talk without being the center of attention, as separate conversations had sprung up. As soon as this happened, a massive arm passed behind Bill and fell upon my shoulder. Gérard was leaning back in his chair and sideward toward me.

"Merlin," he said, "good to see you again. Listen, when you get a chance I'd like to have a little talk with you in private."

"Sure," I said, "but Random and I have to take care of something after dinner."

"When you get a chance," he repeated.

I nodded.

A few moments later I had the feeling that someone was trying to reach me via my Trump.

"Merlin!"

It was Fiona. But she was just sitting at the other end of the table . . .

Her image came clear, however, and I answered her, "Yes?" and then I glanced down the table and saw that she was staring into her handkerchief. She looked up at me then, smiled, and nodded.

I still retained the mental image of her, simultaneously, and I heard it say, *"I dislike raising my voice, for a number of reasons. I'm certain that you will be rushed off after dinner, and I just wanted to let you know that we ought to take a walk, or row out on one of the ponds, or Trump out to Cabra or go look at the Pattern together sometime soon. You understand?"*

"I understand," I said. "I'll be in touch."

"Excellent."

The contact was broken then, and when I glanced her way she was folding her handkerchief and studying her plate.

Random did not linger, but rose quickly after he had finished his dessert, bidding the others a good night and gesturing for Martin and me to accompany him as he departed.

Julian brushed by me on the way out, trying to look somewhat less than sinister and almost succeeding.

"We must go riding together in Arden," he said, "soon."

"Good idea," I told him. "I'll be in touch."

We departed the dining room. Flora caught me in the hall. She still had Bill in tow.

"Stop by my room for a nightcap," she said, "before you turn in. Or come by for tea tomorrow."

"Thank you," I said. "We'll get together. It all depends on how things run, as to just when."

She nodded and hit me with the smile that had caused numerous duels and Balkan crises in the past. Then she moved on and we did too.

As we mounted the stair on the way to the library, Random asked, "Is that everyone?"

"What do you mean?" I said.

"Have they all set up assignations with you by now?"

"Well, they're all tentative things, but yes."

He laughed. "Didn't think they'd waste any time. You'll get everybody's pet suspicions that way. Might as well collect them. Some might come in handy later. They're probably all looking for allies, too—and you should seem a pretty safe choice."

"I do want to visit with all of them. It's just a shame it has to be this way."

He gestured as we came to the top of the stairs. We turned up the hallway and headed toward the library.

"Where are we going?" Martin asked.

Although he resembled Random, Martin looked a little less sneaky, and he was taller. Still, he was not a really big guy.

"To pick up a rifle," Random said.

"Oh? Why?"

"I want to test some ammo Merlin brought back. If it actually fires, our lives have just acquired an additional complication."

We entered the library. The oil lamps were still burning.

The rifle was standing in a corner. Random went to it, dug the shell out of his pocket, and loaded it.

"Okay. What should we try it on?" he mused.

He stepped back out into the hall and looked around.

"Ah! Just the thing!"

He shouldered it, aimed at a suit of armor up the hall, and squeezed the trigger. There followed a sharp report and the ringing of metal. The armor shook.

"Holy shit!" Random said. "It worked! Why me, Unicorn? I was looking for a peaceful reign."

"May I try it, father," Martin asked. "I've always wanted to."

"Why not?" Random said. "You still got that other round, Merlin?"

"Yes," I said, and I rummaged about in my pocket and brought out two. I passed them to Random. "One of these shouldn't work, anyway," I said. "It just got mixed in with the other two."

"All right."

Random accepted both, loaded one. He passed the weapon to Martin then and began explaining its operation. In the distance I heard the sounds of alarm.

"We're about to have the entire palace guard descend upon us," I observed.

"Good," Random answered, as Martin raised the piece to his shoulder. "A little realistic drill every now and then never hurts."

The rifle roared and the armor rang a second time. Martin looked startled and quickly passed the weapon back to Random. Random glanced at the shell in his hand, said, "What the hell!", loaded the final round and fired without sighting.

There was a third report, followed by sounds of a ricochet, just as the guard reached the top of the stair.

"I guess I just don't live right," Random remarked.

After Random had thanked the guard for their prompt response to a training exercise and I overheard a mutter

about the king being in his cups, we returned to the library
and he asked me the question.

"I found the third one in the pocket of Luke's field jacket,"
I answered, and I proceeded to explain the circumstances.

"I can no longer afford *not* to know about Luke Raynard,"
he finally said. "Tell me how you read what just happened."

"The building that burned down," I began. "Upstairs was
Melman who wanted to sacrifice me. Downstairs was the
Brutus Storage Company. Brutus apparently was storing
ammo of this sort. Luke admitted that he knew Melman. I
had no idea that there might be some connection with Brutus
and the ammunition, also. The fact that they were located
in the same building is too much, though."

"If they're turning it out in such quantities that it requires
warehousing, then we're in big trouble," Random said. "I
want to know who owned that building—and who owned
the company, if it's a different person."

"It shouldn't be too difficult to check."

"Who should I send to do it?" he mused. Then he snapped
his fingers and smiled. "Flora is about to undertake an
important mission for the Crown."

"Inspired," I said.

Martin smiled at that and then shook his head. "I'm afraid
I don't understand what's going on," he told us, "and I want
to."

"Tell you what," Random said. "You fill him in while I
go give Flora her assignment. She can leave right after the
funeral."

"Yes," I said as he departed, and I began telling my tale
once again, editing for brevity.

Martin had no fresh insights and no new information,
not that I had expected any of him. He had spent the past
few years off in a more pastoral setting, I learned. I got the
impression that he was more fond of the countryside than
of cities.

"Merlin," he said. "You should have brought this whole
mess home to Amber sooner. We're all affected."

And what of the Courts of Chaos? I wondered. Would

that rifle have fired there? Still, it had been Caine and Bleys who had been targets. No one had summoned me back to the Courts to brief me on any incidents. Still . . . perhaps I ought to bring my other relatives aboard at some point.

"But up until a few days ago matters were a lot simpler," I told Martin, "and then when things began developing fast I was too caught up in them."

"But all those years . . . those attempts on your life . . ."

I said, "I don't call home whenever I stub my toe. Nobody else does either. I couldn't see any connection, all that time."

But I knew that he was right and I was wrong. Fortunately, Random returned about then.

"I couldn't quite get her to believe it was an honor," he said, "but she'll do it."

We talked for a while then about more general matters, mostly what we had been doing for the past several years. I recalled Random's curiosity about Ghostwheel and mentioned the project to him. He changed the subject immediately, giving the impression he wanted to save it for a fully private conversation. After a time, Martin began to yawn and it was contagious. Random decided to bid us good night and rang for a servant to show me to my room.

I asked Dik, who had led me to my quarters, to find me some drawing materials. It took him about ten minutes to turn up everything that I needed.

It would have been a long, difficult walk back and I was tired. So I seated myself beside a table and commenced the construction of a Trump for the bar at the country club Bill had taken me to the previous evening. I worked for perhaps twenty minutes before I was satisfied.

Now it was just a matter of time differential, a thing that was subject to variation, the 2.5-to-1 ratio being only a rule of thumb between Amber and the shadow I had recently inhabited. It was quite possible that I had missed my rendezvous with the nameless housebreaker.

I set everything aside except for the Trump. I rose to my feet.

There came a knock on my door. I was tempted not to

answer it, but my curiosity won out. I crossed the room, unbolted the door, and opened it.

Fiona stood there, her hair down for a change. She had on an attractive green evening dress and a small jeweled pin that matched her hair perfectly.

"Hello, Fi," I said. "What brings you around?"

"I felt you working with certain forces," she answered, "and I didn't want anything happening to you before we had our talk. May I come in?"

"Of course," I said, stepping aside. "But I am in a hurry."

"I know, but perhaps I can be of help."

"How?" I asked, closing the door.

She looked about the room and spotted the Trump I'd just finished. She shot the bolt on the door and crossed to the table.

"Very nice," she observed, studying my handiwork. "So that's where you're headed? Where is it?"

"The bar at a country club in the place I just came from," I replied. "I'm supposed to meet an unknown party there at ten, local time. Hopefully, I will obtain information as to who has been trying to kill me, and why, and possibly even learn something of other matters that have been troubling me."

"Go," she said, "and leave the Trump behind. That way, I can use it to spy, and if you should suddenly need help I will be in a position to provide it."

I reached out and squeezed her hand. Then I took up a position beside the table and focused my attention.

After several moments, the scene took on depth and color. I sank into the emerging textures, and everything advanced toward me, growing larger, crowding out my immediate surroundings. My gaze sought the wall clock I remembered, to the right of the bar...

9:48. I couldn't have cut things much closer.

I could see the patrons now, hear the sounds of their voices. I looked for the best point of arrival. Actually, there was no one at the right end of the bar, near that clock. Okay...

I was there. Trying to look as if I had been, all along. Three of the patrons snapped glances in my direction. I smiled and nodded. Bill had introduced me to one of the men the previous evening. The other I had seen, but not spoken with at that time. Both of them returned my nod, which seemed to satisfy the third that I was real, as he immediately turned his attention back to the woman he was with.

Shortly, the bartender came up to me. He recalled me from last night, also, because he asked whether Bill was around.

I had a beer from him and retired with it to the most secluded table, where I sat and nursed it, my back to the wall, glancing occasionally at the clock, watching the room's two entrances between times. If I tried I could feel Fiona's presence.

Ten o'clock came and went. So did a few patrons, new and old. None of them seemed particularly interested in me, though my own attention was drawn to an unescorted young lady with pale hair and a cameolike profile, which ends the resemblance because cameos don't smile much and she did the second time she glanced at me, right before she looked away. Damn, I thought, why did I have to be wrapped up in a life-and-death situation? Under almost any other circumstances I would have finished the beer, walked over for another, passed a few pleasantries, then asked her whether she'd care to join me. In fact . . .

I glanced at the clock.

10:20.

How much longer should I give the mystery voice? Should I just assume it had been George Hensen, and that he'd given up on tonight when he'd seen me fade? How much longer might the lady hang around?

I growled softly. Stick to business. I studied the narrowness of her waist, the swell of her hips, the tension of her shoulders . . .

10:25.

I noticed that my mug was empty. I took it over for a refill. Dutifully, I watched the progress of the mug.

"I saw you sitting there," I heard her say. "Waiting for someone?"

She smelled strongly of a strange perfume.

"Yes," I said. "But I'm beginning to think it's too late."

"I've a similar problem," she said, and I turned toward her. She was smiling again. "We could wait together," she concluded.

"Please join me," I said. "I'd much rather pass the time with you."

She picked up her drink and followed me back to the table.

"My name's Merle Corey," I told her, as soon as we were seated.

"I'm Meg Devlin. I haven't seen you around before."

"I'm just visiting. You, I take it, are not?"

She shook her head slightly.

"Afraid not. I live in the new apartment complex a couple of miles up the road."

I nodded as if I knew where it was located.

"Where are you from?" she wanted to know.

"The center of the universe," I said, then hastily added, "San Francisco."

"Oh, I've spent a lot of time there. What do you do?"

I resisted a sudden impulse to tell her that I was a sorcerer, and instead described my recent employment at Grand Design. She, I learned in turn, had been a model, a buyer for a large store, and later manager of a boutique.

I glanced at the clock. It was 10:45. She caught the look.

"I think we've both been stood up," she said.

"Probably," I agreed, "but we ought to give them till eleven to be decent about it."

"I suppose."

"Have you eaten?"

"Earlier."

"Hungry?"

"Some. Yes. Are you?"

"Uh-huh, and I noticed some people had food in here earlier. I'll check."

I learned we could get sandwiches, so we got two, with some salad on the side.

"I hope your date didn't include a late supper," I said suddenly.

"It wasn't mentioned, and I don't care," she replied, taking a bite.

Eleven o'clock came and went. I'd finished my drink and the food, and I didn't really want another.

"At least the evening wasn't a total loss," she said, crumpling her napkin and setting it aside.

I watched her eyelashes because it was a pleasant thing to do. She wore very little or very pale makeup. It didn't matter at all. I was about to reach out and cover her hand with my own, but she beat me.

"What were you going to do tonight?" I asked her.

"Oh, dance a bit, have a few drinks, maybe take a walk in the moonlight. Silly things like that."

"I hear music in the next room. We could stroll on over."

"Yes, we could," she said. "Why don't we?"

As we were leaving the bar, I heard Fiona, like a whisper: *"Merlin! If you leave the scene on the Trump you will be out of range to me."*

"Hold on a minute," I answered.

"What?" Meg asked me.

"Uh—I want to visit the rest room first," I said.

"Good idea. I'll do the same. Meet you in the hall here in a couple of minutes."

The place was vacant, but I took a stall in case anyone wandered in. I located Fiona's Trump in the packet I carried. Moments later, I reached Fiona.

"Listen, Fi," I said. "Obviously, no one's going to show. But the rest of the evening promises to shape up nicely, and I might as well have a little fun while I'm here. So thanks for your help. I'll just wander on back later."

"I don't know," she said. *"I don't like you going with*

a stranger, under the circumstances. There may still be danger around there for you, somewhere."

"There isn't," I replied. "I have a way of knowing, and it doesn't register for her. Besides, I'm sure it was a fellow I'd met here and that he gave up when I trumped out. I'll be all right."

"I don't like it," she said.

"I'm a big boy. I can take care of myself."

"I suppose so. Call me immediately if there are any problems."

"There won't be. You might as well turn in."

"And call when you're ready to come back. Don't worry about waking me. I want to bring you home personally."

"Okay, I'll do that. Good night."

"Stay wary."

"I always am."

"Good night, then."

She broke the contact.

A few minutes later we were on the dance floor, turning and listening and touching. Meg had a strong tendency to lead. But what the hell, I can be led. I even tried being wary occasionally but there was nothing more threatening than loud music and sudden laughter.

At eleven-thirty we checked the bar. There were several couples there, but her date wasn't. And no one even gave me a nod. We returned to the music.

We looked again a little after midnight with similar results. We seated ourselves then and ordered a final drink.

"Well, it was fun," she said, resting her hand where I could cover it with my own. So I did.

"Yes," I replied. "I wish we could do it more often. But I'm going to be leaving tomorrow."

"Where are you headed?"

"Back to the center of the universe."

"A pity," she said. "Do you need a ride anywhere?"

I nodded. "Anywhere you're going."

She smiled and squeezed my hand.

"All right," she agreed. "Come on over and I'll make you a cup of coffee."

We finished our drinks and headed out to the parking lot, pausing a few times to embrace along the way. I even tried being wary again, but we seemed to be the only people in the lot. Her car was a neat little red Porsche convertible with the top down.

"Here we are. You care to drive?" she asked.

"No, you do it and I'll watch for headless horsemen."

"What?"

"It's a lovely night, and I've always wanted a chauffeur who looked exactly like you."

We got in and she drove. Fast, of course. It just seemed to follow. The roads were deserted and a feeling of exhilaration swept over me. I raised one hand and summoned a lighted cigar from Shadow. I took a few puffs and tossed it away as we roared over a bridge. I regarded the constellations, which had grown familiar to me these past eight years. I drew a deep breath and let it out slowly. I tried to analyze my feelings and realized that I was happy. I hadn't felt that way in a long while.

A mess of light occurred beyond a fringe of trees up ahead. A minute later we rounded a curve and I saw that it came from a small apartment complex off to the right. She slowed and turned there when we reached it.

She parked in a numbered slot, from whence we made our way along a shrub-lined walk to the building's entrance. She let us in and we crossed the lobby to the elevators. The ride up was over too soon, and once we reached her apartment she really did make coffee.

Which was fine with me. It was good coffee, and we sat together and sipped it. Plenty of time . . .

One thing finally did lead to another. We found ourselves in the bedroom a bit later, our clothes on a nearby chair, and I was congratulating myself that the meeting for which I had returned had not come off. She was smooth and soft and warm, and there was just enough of her in all the right places. A vise in velvet, with honey . . . the scent of her perfume . . .

We lay there, much later, in that peaceful state of temporary fatigue on which I will not waste metaphors. I was stroking her hair when she stretched, turned her head slightly, and regarded me through half-lidded eyes.

"Tell me something," she said.

"Sure."

"What was your mother's name?"

I felt as if something prickly had just been rolled along my spine. But I wanted to see where this was leading. "Dara," I told her.

"And your father?"

"Corwin."

She smiled.

"I thought so," she said, "but I had to be sure."

"Do I get some questions now? Or can only one play?"

"I'll save you the trouble. You want to know why I asked."

"You're on the ball."

"Sorry," she said, moving her leg.

"I take it their names mean something to you?"

"You are Merlin," she stated, "Duke of Kolvir and Prince of Chaos."

"Damn!" I observed. "It seems everybody in this shadow knows who I am! Do you all belong to a club or something?"

"Who else knows?" she asked quickly, her eyes suddenly wide.

"A fellow named Luke Raynard, a dead man named Dan Martinez, a local man named George Hansen, probably— and another dead man named Victor Melman . . . Why? These name ring any bells?"

"Yes, the dangerous one is Luke Raynard. I brought you here to warn you about him, if you were the right one."

"What do you mean 'the right one'?"

"If you were who you are—the son of Dara."

"So warn me."

"I just did. Don't trust him."

I sat up and propped a pillow behind me.

"What's he after? My stamp collection? My traveler's checks? Could you be a little more specific?"

"He tried several times to kill you, years ago—"

"What? How?"

"The first time it involved a truck that almost ran you down. Then the next year—"

"Gods! You really do know! Give me the dates, the dates he tried it."

"April 30, always April 30."

"Why? Do you know why?"

"No."

"Shit. How do you know all of this?"

"I was around. I was watching."

"Why didn't you do something about it?"

"I couldn't. I didn't know which of you was which."

"Lady, you've lost me completely. Who the hell are you, and what's your part in this?"

"Like Luke, I am not what I seem," she began.

There came a sharp buzzing around from the next room.

"Oh my!" she said and sprang out of bed.

I followed her, arriving in the foyer as she pushed a button beside a small grating and said, "Hello?"

"Honey, it's me," came the reply. "I got home a day early. Buzz me in, will you? I'm carrying a bunch of packages."

Oh-oh.

She released the one button and pushed another, turning toward me as she did so.

"The husband," she said, suddenly breathless. "You've got to leave now. Please! Take the steps!"

"But you haven't told me anything yet!"

"I've told you enough. Please don't make trouble!"

"Okay," I said, hurrying back to the bedroom, pulling on my pants and slipping my feet into my loafers.

I stuffed my socks and underwear into my hip pockets and drew on my shirt.

"I'm not satisfied," I said. "You know more and I want it."

"Is that all you want?"

I kissed her cheek quickly.

"Not really. I'll be back," I said.

"Don't," she told me. "It won't be the same. We shall meet again, when the time is right."

I headed for the door.

"That's not good enough," I said as I opened it.

"It will have to be."

"We'll see."

I tore off up the hall and pushed open the door beneath the EXIT sign. I buttoned my shirt and tucked it in on my way down the steps. I paused at the bottom to draw on my socks. I ran a hand through my hair then and opened the door to the lobby.

No one in sight. Good.

As I left the building and headed down the walk a black sedan pulled up in front of me and I heard the hum of a power window and saw a flash of red.

"Get in, Merlin," came a familiar voice.

"Fiona!"

I opened the door and slid inside. We began moving immediately.

"Well, was she?" she asked me.

"Was she what?" I said.

"The one you went to the club to meet."

I hadn't thought of it that way until she said it.

"You know," I said a little later. "I think maybe she was."

She turned onto the road and drove back in the direction from which we had come earlier.

"What kind of game was she playing?" Fiona asked.

"I'd give a lot to know," I answered.

"Tell me about it," she said, "and feel free to edit certain portions."

"Well, all right," I said, and I let her have it.

We were back in the country club parking lot before I was finished.

"Why are we here again?" I asked.

"This is where I got the car. It might belong to a friend of Bill's. I thought I'd be nice and bring it back."

"You used the Trump I'd made to go through to the bar in there?" I asked, gesturing.

"Yes, right after you went in to dance. I watched you for about an hour, mostly from the terrace. And I'd told you to be wary."

"Sorry, I was smitten."

"I'd forgotten they don't serve absinthe here. I had to make do with a frozen marguerita."

"Sorry about that, too. Then you hot-wired a car and followed us when we left?"

"Yes. I waited in her parking lot and maintained the most peripheral of touches with you via your Trump. If I'd felt danger I would have come in after you."

"Thanks. How peripheral?"

"I am not a voyeur, if that's what you mean. Very well, we're up to date."

"There's a lot more to the story than this last part."

"Keep it," she said, "for now. There is only one thing I am curious about at the moment. Would you happen to have a picture of this Luke Raynard?"

"I might," I told her, reaching for my wallet. "Yes, I think I do."

I withdrew my shorts from my hip pocket and explored further.

"At least you don't wear jockeys," she remarked.

I withdrew my wallet and turned on the overhead light. As I flipped the wallet open she leaned toward me, resting her hand on my arm. Finally, I found a clear colored photo of Luke and me at the beach, with Julia and a girl named Gail whom Luke used to date.

I felt her grip tighten as she drew in a short, sharp breath.

"What is it?" I asked. "You know him?"

She shook her head too quickly.

"No. No," she said. "Never saw him before in my life."

"You're a lousy liar, Auntie. Who is it?"

"I don't know," she said.

"Come on! You nearly broke my arm when you saw him."

"Don't push me," she said.

"It involves my life."

"It involves more than your life, I think."

"So?"

"Let it be, for now."

"I'm afraid I can't do that. I must insist."

She turned more fully and both of her hands came up between us. Smoke began to rise from her well-manicured fingertips. Frakir throbbed upon my wrist, which meant she was sufficiently pissed off to lean on me if it came to that.

I made a warding gesture and decided to back off.

"Okay, let's call it a day and head home."

She flexed her fingers and the smoke fled. Frakir became still. She withdrew a packet of Trumps from her purse and shuffled out the one for Amber.

"But sooner or later I'm going to have to know," I added.

"Later," she said, as the vision of Amber grew before us.

One thing I always liked about Fiona: she didn't believe in hiding her feelings.

I reached up and switched off the dome light as Amber came on all around us.

CHAPTER 8

I guess that my thoughts at funerals are typical. Like Bloom in *Ulysses,* I think the most mundane things about the deceased and the current goings-on. The rest of the time my mind wanders.

On the wide strand of shoreline at the southern foot of Kolvir there is a small chapel dedicated to the Unicorn, one of several such throughout the realm at places where she had been sighted. This one seemed most appropriate for Caine's service in that—like Gérard—he had once expressed a desire to be laid to rest in one of the sea caves at the mountain's foot, facing the waters he had sailed so long, so often. One such had been prepared for him, and there would be a procession after the service to inter him there. It was a windy, misty, sea-cool morning with only a few sails in sight, moving to or from the port over half a league westward of us.

Technically, I suppose Random should have officiated, since his kingship automatically made him high priest, but aside from reading an opening and closing passage on the Passing of Princes from the Book of the Unicorn, he turned

the service over to Gérard to perform in his stead, as Caine
had gotten along with Gérard better than with anyone else
in the family. So Gérard's booming voice filled the small
stone building, reading long sections involving the sea and
mutability. It was said that Dworkin himself had penned the
Book in his saner days, and that long passages had come
direct from the Unicorn. I don't know. I wasn't there. It is
also said that we are descended of Dworkin and the Unicorn,
which gives rise to some unusual mental images. Origins
of anything tend to fade off into myth, though. Who knows?
I wasn't around then.

   ". . . And all things return to the sea," Gérard was saying.
I looked about me. Besides the family, there were perhaps
forty or fifty people present, mostly nobility from the town,
a few merchants with whom Caine had been friendly, rep-
resentatives of realms in several adjacent shadows where
Caine had spent time on both official and personal business,
and of course Vinta Bayle. Bill had expressed a desire to
be present, and he stood to my left. Martin was at my right.
Neither Fiona nor Bleys was present. Bleys had pleaded his
injury and excused himself from the service. Fiona had
simply vanished. Random had been unable to locate her this
morning. Julian departed partway through the service, to
check on the guard he had posted along the strand, someone
having pointed out that a would-be assassin could rack up
a high score with that many of us together in one small
space. Consequently, Julian's foresters, with short sword,
dagger, and longbow or lance, were spotted strategically all
over the place—and every now and then we'd hear the
baying of one of his hellhounds, to be answered almost
immediately by several others, a mournful, unnerving thing,
counterpointing waves, wind, and reflections upon mortal-
ity. Where had she gotten off to? I wondered. Fiona? Fear
of a trap? Or something to do with last night? And Benedict
. . . he had sent regrets and regards, mentioning sudden business that precluded his making it back in time. Llewella
simply hadn't shown, and could not be reached by Trump.
Flora stood ahead and to the left of me, knowing she looked

lovely in dark colors, too. Perhaps I do her an injustice. I don't know. But she seemed more fidgety than contemplative.

At the conclusion of the service we filed out, four seamen bearing Caine's casket, and we formed up into a procession that would lead to the cave and his sarcophagus. A number of Julian's troops came up to pace us as an armed escort.

As we walked along, Bill nudged me and gestured upward with his head, toward Kolvir. I looked in that direction and beheld a black-cloaked and cowled figure standing upon a ledge in the shadow of a rocky projection. Bill leaned close so that I could hear him above the sound of the pipes and strings that were now playing.

"Is that one some part of the ceremony?" he asked.

"Not that I know of," I answered.

I broke out of line and moved forward. In another minute or so we would pass directly beneath the figure.

I caught up with Random and put my hand on his shoulder. When he looked back I pointed upward. He halted and stared, squinting.

His right hand rose to his breast, where he wore the Jewel of Judgment, as on most state occasions. Instantly, the winds rose.

"Halt!" Random called out. "Stop the procession! Everyone stay where you are!"

The figure moved then, slightly, head turning as if to stare at Random. In the sky, as if by trick photography, a cloud blew itself together, growing, above Kolvir. A red, pulsing glow emerged from beneath Random's hand.

Suddenly, the figure looked upward and a hand flashed beneath the cloak, emerging moments later to perform a quick casting movement. A tiny black object hung in the air, then began its descent.

"Everybody down!" Gérard called out.

Random did not move as the others of us dropped. He remained standing, watching, as lightning emerged from the cloud and played across the face of the cliff.

The thunder that followed coincided almost exactly with

the explosion that occurred high overhead. The distance had been too great. The bomb had gone off before it reached us—though it would probably have scored had we continued as we were, to pass beneath the ledge and have it dropped directly upon us. When the spots stopped dancing before my eyes, I regarded the cliff again. The dark figure was gone.

"Did you get him?" I asked Random.

He shrugged as he lowered his hand. The Jewel had ceased its pulsing.

"Everybody on your feet!" he called out. "Let's get on with this funeral!"

And we did. There were no more incidents, and the business was concluded as planned.

My thoughts, and probably everyone else's, were already playing family games as the box was being fitted into the vault. Might the attacker have been one of our absent kin? And if so, which one? What motives might each of them possess for the act? Where were they now? And what were their alibis? Could there have been a coalition involved? Or could it have been an outsider? If so, how was access obtained to the local supply of explosives? Or was this imported stuff? Or had someone local come up with the proper formula? If it were an outsider, what was the motive and where was the person from? Had one of us imported an assassin? Why?

As we filed past the vault I did think fleetingly of Caine, but more as part of the puzzle picture than as an individual. I had not known him all that well. But then, several of the others had told me early on that he was not the easiest person to get to know. He was tough and cynical and had a streak of cruelty in his nature. He had made quite a few enemies over the years and seemed even to be proud of this fact. He had always been decent enough with me, but then we'd never been at cross-purposes over anything. So my feelings did not run as deep for him as they did for most of the others. Julian was another of this cut, but more polished on the surface. And no one could be certain what lay beneath that surface on any given day. Caine . . . I wish I'd gotten to know you better. I am certain that I am diminished by your passing in ways that I do not even understand.

Departing, afterward, heading back to the palace for food and drink, I wondered, not for the first time, how my problems and everyone else's were connected. For I felt they were. I don't mind small coincidences, but I don't trust big ones.

And Meg Devlin? Did she know something of this business, too? It seemed possible that she might. Husband or no husband, I decided, we had a date. Soon.

Later, in the big dining hall, amid the buzz of conversation and the rattle of cutlery and crockery, one vague possibility occurred to me and I resolved to pursue it immediately. Excusing myself from the cold but attractive company of Vinta Bayle, third daughter of some minor nobility and apparently Caine's last mistress, I made my way to the far end of the hall and the small knot of people surrounding Random. I was standing there for several minutes, wondering how to break in, when he spotted me. He excused himself from the others immediately, advanced upon me, and caught hold of my sleeve.

"Merlin," he said, "I don't have time now, but I just wanted to let you know that I don't consider our conversation concluded. I want to get together with you again later this afternoon or this evening—as soon as I'm free. So don't go running off anywhere till we've talked, okay?"

I nodded.

"One quick question," I said, as he began turning back toward the others.

"Shoot," he said.

"Are there any Amberites currently in residence on the shadow Earth I just departed—agents of any sort?"

He shook his head.

"I don't have any, and I don't believe any of the others do just now. I have a number of contacts there in different places, but they're all natives—like Bill."

His eyes narrowed. "Something new come up?" he asked
then.

I nodded again.

"Serious?"

"Possibly."

"I wish I had the time to hear it, but it'll just have to
keep till we talk later."

"I understand."

"I'll send for you," he said, and he returned to his com-
panions.

That shot down the only explanation I could think of for
Meg Devlin. It also foreclosed the possibility of my taking
off to see her as soon as I could leave the gathering.

I consoled myself with another plate of food. After a
time, Flora entered the hall, studied all the knots of human-
ity, then made her way among them to settle beside me on
the window seat.

"No way of talking to Random right now without an
audience," she said.

"You're right," I replied. "May I get you something to
eat or drink?"

"Not now. Maybe you can help. You're a sorcerer."

I didn't like that opening, but I asked, "What's the problem?"

"I went to Bleys' rooms, to see whether he wanted to
come down and join us. He's gone."

"Wasn't his door locked? Most people do that around
here."

"Yes, from the inside. So he must have trumped out. I
broke in when he didn't answer, since there'd been one
attempt on his life already."

"And what would you want of a sorcerer?"

"Can you trace him?"

"Trumps don't leave tracks," I said. "But even if I could,
I'm not so sure that I would. He knows what he's doing,
and he obviously wants to be left alone."

"But what if he's involved? He and Caine had been on
opposite sides in the past."

"If he's mixed up in something dangerous to the rest of us you should be happy to see him go."

"So you can't help—or won't?"

I nodded. "Both, I guess. Any decision to seek him out should really come from Random, don't you think?"

"Maybe."

"I'd suggest keeping it to yourself till you can talk to Random. No use stirring up fruitless speculations among the others. Or I'll tell him, if you'd like. I'm going to be talking with him a bit later."

"What about?"

Ouch.

"Not sure," I said. "It's something he wants to tell me, or ask me."

She studied me carefully.

"We haven't really had our own little talk yet," she said then.

"Looks like we're having it now."

"Okay. May I hear about your problems in one of my favorite shadows?"

"Why not?" I said, and I launched into a synopsis of the damned thing again. I felt that this would be the final time, though. Once Flora knew it I was confident it would make the rounds.

She had no information bearing upon my case that she cared to share. We chatted for a while then—local gossip—and she finally decided to get something to eat. She departed in the direction of the food and did not return.

I talked with a few of the others, too—about Caine, about my father. I did not hear anything that I did not already know. I was introduced to a number of people I had not met before. I memorized a mess of names and relationships since I had nothing better to do.

When things finally broke up, I kept an eye on Random and contrived to depart at about the same time he did.

"Later," he said as we passed, and he went off with a couple of guys he'd been talking with.

So I went back to my rooms and stretched out on the

bed. When things are brewing you take your rest whenever you can.

After a time I slept, and I dreamed...

I was walking in the formal garden behind the palace. Someone else was with me, but I did not know who it was. This did not seem to matter. I heard a familiar howling. Suddenly, there were growling noises near at hand. The first time I looked about I saw nothing. But then, abruptly, they were there—three huge, doglike creatures similar to the one I had slain in Julia's apartment. They were racing toward me across the garden. The howling continued, but they were not its authors. They restricted themselves to growling and slavering as they came on. Just as suddenly, I realized that this was a dream and that I had dreamt it several times before only to lose track of it upon awakening. The knowledge that it was a dream, however, in no way detracted from the feeling of menace as they rushed toward me. All three of them were surrounded by a kind of light—pale, distorting. Looking past them, through their haloes, I did not see the garden but caught glimpses of a forest. When they drew near and sprang to attack it was as if they had encountered a glass wall. They fell back, rose and dashed toward me once more only to be blocked again. They leaped and growled and whined and tried again. It was as if I stood beneath a bell jar or within a magic circle, though. They could not get at me. Then the howling came louder, came nearer and they turned their attention away from me.

"Wow!" Random said. "I should charge you something for pulling you out of a nightmare."

... And I was awake and lying on my bed and there was darkness beyond my window—and I realized that Random had called me via my Trump and tuned in on my dream when he'd made contact.

I yawned and thought him my answer; *Thanks*.

"Finish waking up and let's have our talk," he said.

"Yes. Where are you?"

"Downstairs. The little sitting room off the main hall to the south. Drinking coffee. We've got it to ourselves."

"See you in five."

"Check."

Random faded. I sat up, swung my feet over the side of the bed, and rose. I crossed the room to the window and flung it wide. I inhaled the crisp evening air of autumn. Spring on the shadow Earth, fall here in Amber—my two favorite seasons. I should be heartened, uplifted. Instead— a trick of the night, the tag-end of the dream—it seemed for a moment that I heard the final note of the howling. I shuddered and closed the window. Our dreams are too much with us.

I hiked down to the designated room and took a seat on one of its sofas. Random let me get through half a cup of coffee before he said, "Tell me about the Ghostwheel."

"It's a kind of—paraphysical surveillance device and library."

Random put down his cup and cocked his head to one side.

"Could you be more specific?" he said.

"Well, my work with computers led me to speculate that basic data-processing principles could be employed with interesting results in a place where computer mechanics themselves would not operate," I began. "In other words, I had to locate a shadow environment where the operations would remain pretty much invariant but where the physical construct, all of the peripherals, the programming techniques and the energy inputs would be of a different nature."

"Uh, Merlin," Random said. "You've lost me already."

"I designed and built a piece of data-processing equipment in a shadow where no ordinary computer could function," I replied, "because I used different materials, a radically different design, a different power source. I also chose a place where different physical laws apply, so that it could operate along different lines. I was then able to write programs for it which would not have operated on the shadow Earth where I'd been living. In doing so, I believe that I created a unique artifact. I called it the Ghostwheel because of certain aspects of its appearance."

"And it's a surveillance device and a library. What do you mean by that?"

"It riffles through Shadow like the pages of a book—or a deck of cards," I said. "Program it for whatever you want checked out and it will keep an eye on it for you. I was planning it as a surprise. You could, say, use it to determine whether any of our potential enemies are mobilizing, or to follow the progress of Shadow-storms, or—"

"Wait a minute," he said, raising a hand. "How? How does it flip through shadows that way? What makes it work?"

"In effect," I explained, "it creates the equivalent of multitudes of Trumps in an instant, then—"

"Stop. Back up. How can you write a program for the creation of Trumps? I thought they could only be done by a person who had an initiate of either the Pattern or the Logrus."

"But in this case," I said, "the machine itself is of that same class of magical objects as Dad's blade, Grayswandir. I incorporated elements of the Pattern itself into its design."

"And you were going to surprise us with this?"

"Yes, once it's ready."

"When will that be?"

"I'm not sure. It had to gather certain critical amounts of data before its programs could become fully operational. I set it to do that a while back, and I haven't had a chance to check on it recently."

Random poured some more coffee, took a drink.

"I don't see where it would save that much in the way of time and effort," he said a little later. "Say I'm curious about something in Shadow. I go and investigate, or I send someone. Now, say that instead I want to use this thing to check it out. I still have to spend the time going to the place where you keep it."

"No," I told him. "You summon a remote terminal."

"Summon? A terminal?"

"Right."

I unearthed my Amber Trumps and dealt myself the one

off the bottom. It showed a silver wheel against a dark background. I passed it to Random and he studied it.

"How do you use it?" he asked.

"Same as the others. You want to call it to you?"

"You do it," he said. "I want to watch."

"Very well," I answered. "But while I've set it to gathering data across the shadows it still won't know a whole lot that's useful at this point."

"I don't want to question it so much as I want to see it."

I raised the card and stared, seeing through it with my mind's eye. After a few moments, there was contact. I called it to me.

There followed a small crackling sound and a feeling of ionization in the air as a glowing wheel about eight feet in diameter materialized before me.

"Diminish terminal size," I ordered.

It shrank down to about a third of what it had been and I ordered it to halt at that point. It looked like a pale picture frame, occasional sparks dancing within it, the view across the room constantly rippling as seen through its center.

Random began to extend a hand.

"Don't," I said. "You might get a shock. I still don't have all the bugs out."

"It can transmit energy?"

"Well, it could. No big deal."

"If you ordered to transmit energy . . . ?"

"Oh, sure. It has to be able to transmit energy here to sustain the terminal, and through Shadow to operate its scanners."

"I mean, could it discharge it at this end?"

"If I told it to it could build up a charge and let it go. Yes."

"What are its limits in this?"

"Whatever it has available."

"And what does it have available?"

"Well, in theory an entire planet. But—"

"Supposing you ordered it to appear beside someone

here, build up a large charge and discharge it into that person. Could it do an electrocution?"

"I guess so," I said. "I don't see why not. But that's not its purpose—"

"Merlin, your surprise is certainly a surprise. But I'm not sure I like it."

"It's safe," I explained. "No one knows where it's located. No one goes there. This Trump I have is the only one. Nobody else can reach it. I was going to make one more card, just for you, and then show you how to operate the thing when it was ready."

"I'm going to have to think about this . . ."

"Ghost, within five thousand Shadow veils, this location—how many Shadow-storms are currently in existence?"

The words came as if spoken within the hoop: "Seventeen."

"Sounds like—"

"I gave it my voice," I told him. "Ghost, give us some pictures of the biggest one."

A scene of chaotic fury filled the hoop.

"Another thought just occurred to me," Random stated. "Can it transport things?"

"Sure, just like a regular Trump."

"Was the original size of that circle its maximum size?"

"No, we could make it a lot larger if you wanted. Or smaller."

"I don't. But supposing you made it larger—and then told it to transmit that storm, or as much of it as it could manage?"

"Wow! I don't know. It would try. It would probably be like opening a giant window onto it."

"Merlin, shut it down. It's dangerous."

"Like I said, nobody knows where it is but me, and the only other way to reach it is—"

"I know, I know. Tell me, could anybody access it with the proper Trump, or just by finding it?"

"Well, yes. I didn't bother with any security codes because of its inaccessibility."

"That thing could be an awesome weapon, kid. Shut it down. Now."

"I can't."

"What do you mean?"

"You can't dump its memory or kill its power from a remote terminal. I would actually have to travel to the site itself to do that."

"Then I suggest you get going. I want it turned off until there are a lot more safeguards built into it. Even then —well, we'll see. I don't trust a power like that. Not when I don't have any defenses against it. It could strike almost without warning. What were you thinking of when you built that thing?"

"Data-processing. Look, we're the only ones—"

"There's always a possibility someone will get wise to it and find a way to get at it. I know, I know—you're in love with your handiwork—and I appreciate what you had in mind. But it's got to go."

"I have done nothing to offend you." It was my voice, but it came from the wheel.

Random stared at it, looked at me, looked back at it.

"Uh—that's not the point," he addressed it. "It's your potential that I'm concerned about.

"Merlin, turn off the terminal!"

"End transmission," I said. "Withdraw terminal."

It wavered a moment, then was gone.

"Had you anticipated that comment from the thing?" Random asked me.

"No. I was surprised."

"I'm beginning to dislike surprises. Maybe that shadow environment is actually altering the thing in subtle ways. You know my wishes. Give it a rest."

I bowed my head. "Whatever you say, sir."

"Cut it out. Don't be a martyr. Just do it."

"I still think it's just a matter of installing a few safeguards. No reason to crash the whole project."

"If things were quieter," he said, "maybe I'd go along with it. But there's too much shit coming down right now, with snipers and bombers and all the things you've been telling me about. I don't need another worry."

I got to my feet. "Okay. Thanks for the coffee," I said. "I'll let you know when it's done."

He nodded. "Good night, Merlin."

"Good night."

As I was stalking out through the big entrance hall I saw Julian, in a green dressing gown, talking with two of his men. On the floor between them lay a large dead animal. I halted and stared. It was one of those same damned dog things I had just dreamed about, like at Julia's.

I approached. "Hi, Julian. What is it?" I asked gesturing.

He shook his head. "Don't know. But the hellhounds just killed three of them in Arden. I trumped these guys up with one of the carcasses, to show Random. You wouldn't know where he is, would you?"

I stabbed with my thumb back over my shoulder. "In the sitting room."

He walked off in that direction. I went nearer and prodded the animal with my toe. Should I go back and tell Random I'd met one before?

The hell with it, I decided. I couldn't see how the information would be of any vital use.

I returned to my rooms and washed up and changed my clothes. Then I stopped by the kitchen and filled my backpack with food. I didn't feel like saying good-bye to anyone, so I just headed for the back and took the big rear staircase down into the gardens.

Dark. Starry. Cool. Walking, I felt a sudden chill as I neared the spot where, in my dream, the dogs had appeared.

No howls, no growls. Nothing. I passed through that area and continued on my way to the rear of that well-kept site, to the place where a number of trails led off through a more natural landscape. I took the second one from the left. It was a slightly longer route than another I might have chosen—with which it intersected later, anyway—but was easier going, a thing I felt I needed in the night. I was still not all that familiar with the irregularities of the other way.

I hiked the crest of Kolvir for the better part of an hour before I located the downward trail I was seeking. I halted then, took a drink of water and rested for a few minutes before I began the descent.

It is very difficult to walk in Shadow on Kolvir. One has to put some distance between oneself and Amber in order to do it properly. So all I could do at this point was hike— which was fine with me, because it was a good night for walking.

I was well on my way down before a glow occurred overhead and the moon crested a shoulder of Kolvir and poured its light upon my twisting trail. I increased my pace somewhat after that. I did want to make it off the mountain by morning.

I was angry with Random for not giving me a chance to justify my work. I hadn't really been ready to tell him about it. If it hadn't been for Caine's funeral I would not have returned to Amber until I'd had the thing perfected. And I wasn't even going to mention Ghostwheel this time around, except that it had figured in a small way in the mystery that had engulfed me and Random had wanted to know about it in order to have the whole story. Okay. He didn't like what he'd seen, but the preview had been premature. Now, if I shut it down as I'd been ordered I would ruin a lot of work that had been in progress for some time now. Ghostwheel was still in a Shadow-scanning, self-education phase. I would have been checking on it about now, anyway, to see how it was coming along and to correct any obvious flaws that had crept into the system.

I thought about it as the trail grew steeper and curved on Kolvir's western face. Random had not exactly ordered me to dump everything it had accumulated thus far. He'd simply told me to shut it down. Viewed the way I chose to view it, that meant I could exercise my own judgment as to means. I decided that gave me leeway to check everything out first, reviewing systems functions and revising programs until I was satisfied that everything was in order. Then I could transfer everything to a more permanent status before shutting it down. Then nothing would be lost; its memory would be intact when the time came to restore its functions again.

Maybe . . .

What if I did everything to make it shipshape, including throwing in a few—as I saw it—unnecessary safeguards to make Random happy? Then, I mused, supposing I got in touch with Random, showed him what I'd done, and asked him whether he was happy with it that way? If he weren't, I could always shut it down then. But perhaps he'd reconsider. Worth thinking about . . .

I played over imaginary conversations with Random until the moon had drifted off to my left. I was more than halfway down Kolvir by then and the going was becoming progressively easier. I could already feel the force of the Pattern as somewhat diminished.

I halted a couple of more times on the way down, for water and once for a sandwich. The more I thought about it, the more I felt that Random would just get angry if I proceeded along the lines I had been thinking and probably wouldn't even give me a full hearing. On the other hand, I was angry myself.

But it was a long journey with few shortcuts. I'd have plenty of time to mull it over.

The sky was growing lighter when I crossed the last rocky slope to reach the wide trail at the foot of Kolvir to the northwest. I regarded a stand of trees across the way, one large one a familiar landmark—

With a dazzling flash that seemed to sizzle and a bomb-like report of thunder the tree was split, not a hundred meters away. I'd flung up both hands at the lightning stroke, but I could still hear cracking wood and the echo of the blast for several seconds afterward.

Then a voice cried out, "Go back!"

I assumed I was the subject of this conversational gambit. "May we talk this over?" I responded.

There was no reply.

I stretched out in a shallow declivity beside the trail, then crawled along it for several body lengths to a place where the cover was better. I was listening and watching the while, hoping that whoever had pulled that stunt would betray his position in some fashion.

Nothing happened, but for the next half minute I surveyed the grove and a portion of the slope down which I had come. From that angle their proximity gave me a small inspiration.

I summoned the image of the Logrus, and two of its lines became my arms. I reached then, not through Shadow but up the slope to where a fairly good-sized rock was poised above a mass of others.

Seizing hold, I drew upon it. It was too heavy to topple easily, so I began rocking it. Slowly, at first. Finally, I got it to the tipping point and it tumbled. It fell among the others and a small cascade began. I withdrew further as they struck and sent new ones bouncing. Several big ones began to roll. A fracture line gave way when they fell upon its edge at a steeper place. An entire sheet of stone groaned and cracked, began to slide.

I could feel the vibration as I continued my withdrawal. I had not anticipated setting off anything this spectacular. The rocks bounced, slid and flew into the grove. I watched the trees sway, saw some of them go down. I heard the crunching, the pinging, the breaking.

I gave it an extra half minute after what seemed its end. There was much dust in the air and half of the grove was down. Then I rose to my feet, Frakir dangling from my left hand, and I advanced upon the grove.

I searched carefully, but there was no one there. I climbed upon the trunk of a fallen tree.

"I repeat, do you care to talk about it?" I called out.

No answer.

"Okay, be that way," I said, and I headed north into Arden.

* * *

I heard the sound of horses occasionally as I hiked through that ancient forest. If I was being followed, though, the horsemen showed no interest in closing with me. Most likely, I was passing in the vicinity of one of Julian's patrols.

Not that it mattered. I soon located a trail and began the small adjustments that bore me farther and farther from them.

A lighter shade, from brown to yellow, and slightly shorter trees . . . Fewer breaks in the leafy canopy . . . Odd bird note, strange mushroom . . .

Little by little, the character of the wood was altered. And the shifting grew easier and easier the farther this took me from Amber.

I began to pass sunny clearings. The sky grew a paler blue . . . The trees were all green now, but most of them saplings . . .

I broke into a jog.

Masses of clouds came into view, the spongy earth grew firmer, drier . . .

I stepped up my pace, heading downhill. Grasses were more abundant. The trees were divided into clusters now, islands in a waving sea of those pale grasses. My view took in a greater distance. A flapping, beaded curtain off to my right: rain.

Rumbles of thunder came to me, though sunlight continued to light my way. I breathed deeply of the clean damp air and ran on.

The grasses fell away, ground fissured, sky blackened . . . Waters rushed through canyons and arroyos all about me . . . Torrents poured from overhead onto the rocking terrain . . .

I began slipping. I cursed each time I picked myself up, for my overeagerness in the shifting.

The clouds parted like a theater curtain, to where a lemon sun poured warmth and light from a salmon-colored sky. The thunder halted in mid-rumble and a wind rose . . .

I made my way up a hillside, looked down upon a ruined

village. Long-abandoned, partly overgrown, strange mounds lined its broken main street.

I passed through it beneath a slate-colored sky, picked my way slowly across an icy pond, faces of those frozen beneath me staring sightlessly in all directions . . .

The sky was soot-streaked, the snow hard-packed, my breath feathery as I entered the skeletal wood where frozen birds perched: an etching.

Slipping downhill, rolling, sliding into melting and spring . . . Movement again, about me . . . Mucky ground and clumps of green . . . Strange cars on distant highway . . .

A junkyard, smelling, oozing, rusting, smoldering . . . Threading my way amid acres of heaps . . . Rats scurrying . . .

Away . . . Shifting faster, breathing harder . . . Skyline beneath smog cap . . . Delta bottom . . . Seashore . . . Golden pylons along the road . . . Countryside with lakes . . . Brown grasses beneath green sky . . .

Slowing . . . Rolling grassland, river and lake . . . Slowing . . . Breeze and grass, sealike . . . Mopping my brow on my sleeve . . . Sucking air . . . Walking now . . .

I moved through the field at a normal pace, preferring to do my resting in a congenial spot such as this, where I could see for a good distance. The wind made soft noises as it passed among the grasses. The nearest lake was a deep lime color. Something in the air smelled sweet.

I thought I saw a brief flash of light off to my right, but when I looked that way there was nothing unusual to be seen. A little later, I was certain that I heard a distant sound of hoofbeats. But again, I saw nothing. That's the trouble with shadows—you don't always know what's natural there; you're never certain what to look for.

Several minutes passed, and then I smelled it before I saw anything.

Smoke.

The next instant there was a rush of fire. A long line of flame cut across my path.

And again the voice: "I told you to go back!"

The wind was behind the fire, pushing it toward me. I turned to head away and saw that it was already flanking me. It takes a while to build up the proper mental set for shadow-shifting, and I had let mine go. I doubted I could set it up again in time.

I began running.

The line of flame was curving about me, as if to describe a huge circle. I did not pause to admire the precision of the thing, however, as I could feel the heat by then and the smoke was getting thicker.

Above the fire's crackling it seemed that I could still hear the drumming of hoofs. My eyes were beginning to water, though, and streams of smoke further diminished my vision. And again, I detected no sign of the person who had sprung the trap.

Yet—definitely—the ground was shaking with the rapid progress of a hooved creature headed in my direction. The flames flashed higher, drew nearer as the circle rushed toward closure.

I was wondering what new menace was approaching, when a horse and rider burst into view through the gap in the fiery wall. The rider drew back the reins, but the horse— a chestnut—was not too happy at the nearness of the flames. It bared its teeth, biting at the bit, and tried several times to rear.

"Hurry! Behind me!" the rider cried, and I rushed to mount.

The rider was a dark-haired woman. I caught only a glimpse of her features. She managed to turn the horse back in the direction from which she had come, and she shook the reins. The chestnut started forward, and suddenly it reared. I managed to hang on.

When its front hooves struck the ground, the beast wheeled and tore off toward the light. It was almost into the flames when it wheeled again.

"Damn!" I heard the rider say, as she worked almost frantically with the reins.

The horse turned again, neighing loudly. Bloody spittle

dripped from its mouth. And by then the circle was closed, the smoke was heavy and the flames very near. I was in no position to help, beyond giving it a pair of sharp kicks in the flanks when it began moving in a straight line again.

It plunged into the flames to our left, almost screaming as it went. I had no idea how wide the band of fire was at that point. I could feel a searing along my legs, though, and I smelled burning hair.

Then the beast was roaring again, the rider was screaming back at it, and I found that I could no longer hold on. I felt myself sliding backward just as we broke through the ring of fire and into a charred, smoldering area where the flames had already passed. I fell amid hot black clumps; ashes rose about me. I rolled frantically to my left, and I coughed and squeezed my eyes shut against the cloud of ashes that assailed my face.

I heard the woman scream and I scrambled to my feet, rubbing my eyes. My vision came clear in time for me to see the chestnut rising from where he had apparently fallen atop his rider. The horse immediately tore off, to be lost among clouds of smoke. The woman lay very still and I rushed to her side. Kneeling, I brushed sparks from her clothing and checked for breathing and a pulse. Her eyes opened while I was doing this.

"Back's—broken—I think," she said, coughing. "Don't feel—much. . . . Escape—if you can. . . . Leave me. I'll die—anyway."

"No way," I said. "But I've got to move you. There's a lake nearby, if I remember right."

I removed my cloak where it was tied about my waist and I spread it out beside her. I inched her onto it as carefully as I could, folded it over her to protect her against the flames and began dragging her in what I hoped was the proper direction.

We made it through a shifting patchwork of fire and smoke. My throat was raw, my eyes watering steadily and my trousers on fire when I took a big step backward and felt my heel squish downward into mud. I kept going.

Finally, I was waist deep in the water and supporting her there. I leaned forward, pushed a flap of the cloak back from her face. Her eyes were still open, but they looked unfocused and there was no movement. Before I could feel for a carotid pulse, however, she made a hissing noise, then she spoke my name.

"Merlin," she said hoarsely, "I'm—sorry—"

"You helped me and I couldn't help you," I said. *"I'm sorry."*

"Sorry—I didn't last—longer," she continued. "No good—with horses. They're—following you."

"Who?" I asked.

"Called off—the dogs, though. But the—fire—is—someone—else's. Don't know—whose."

"I don't know what you're talking about."

I splashed a little water onto her cheeks to cool them. Between the soot and her singed, disheveled hair it was difficult to judge her appearance.

"Someone—behind—you," she said, her voice growing fainter. "Someone—ahead—too. Didn't—know—about—that one. Sorry."

"Who?" I asked again. "And who are you? How do you know me? Why—"

She smiled faintly. ". . . Sleep with you. Can't now. Going . . ."

Her eyes closed.

"No!" I cried.

Her face contorted and she sucked in a final breath. She expelled it then, using it to form the whispered words. "Just—let me—sink here. G'bye . . ."

A cloud of smoke blew across her face. I held my breath and shut my eyes as a larger billow followed, engulfing us.

When the air finally cleared again, I studied her. Her breathing had ceased and there was no pulse, no heartbeat. There was no nonburning, nonmarshy area available for even an attempt at CPR. She was gone. She'd known she was going.

I wrapped my cloak about her carefully, turning it into

a shroud. Last of all, I folded a flap over her face. I fixed everything into place with the clasp I'd used to close it at my neck when I'd worn it. Then I waded out into deeper water. "Just let me sink here." Sometimes the dead sink quickly, sometimes they float...

"Good-bye, lady," I said. "Wish I knew your name. Thanks again."

I released my hold upon her. The waters swirled. She was gone. After a time, I looked away then moved away. Too many questions and no answers.

Somewhere, a maddened horse was screaming...

CHAPTER 9

Several hours and many shadows later I rested again, in a place with a clear sky and not much tinder about. I bathed in a shallow stream and afterward summoned fresh clothing out of Shadow. Clean and dry then, I rested on the bank and made myself a meal.

It seemed as if every day were now an April 30. It seemed as if everyone I met knew me, and as if everyone were playing an elaborate double-game. People were dying all about me and disasters were becoming a common occurrence. I was beginning to feel like a figure in a video game. What would be next? I wondered. A meteor shower?

There had to be a key. The nameless lady who had given her life to pull me out of the fire had said that someone was following me and that there was someone ahead of me, also. What did that mean? Should I wait for my pursuer to catch up and simply ask him, her, or it what the hell was going on? Or should I push on fast, hopefully catch the other party and make inquiry there? Would either give me the same answer? Or were there two different answers involved? Would a duel satisfy someone's honor? I'd fight it, then. Or a bribe.

I'd pay it. All I wanted was an answer followed by a little peace and quiet. I chuckled. That sounded like a description of death—though I wasn't that sure about the answer part.

"Shit!" I commented, to no one in particular, and I tossed a stone into the stream.

I got to my feet and crossed the water. Written in the sand on its opposite shore were the words GO BACK. I stepped on them and broke into a run.

The world spun about me as I touched the shadows. Vegetation fell away. The rocks grew into boulders, lightening, taking on a sparkle...

I ran through a valley of prisms beneath an awesome purple sky... Wind among rainbow stones, singing, Aeolian music...

Garments lashed by gales... Purple to lavender above ... Sharp cries within the strains of sound... Earth cracking...

Faster.

I am giant. Same landscape, infinitesimal now... Cyclopean, I grind the glowing stones beneath my feet... Dust of rainbows upon my boots, puffs of cloud about my shoulders...

Atmosphere thickening, thickening, almost to liquid, and green... Swirling... Slow motion, my best efforts...

Swimming in it... Castles fit for aquaria drift by... Bright missiles like fireflies assail me... I feel nothing...

Green to blue... Thinning, thinning... Blue smoke and air like incense... The reverberation of a million invisible gongs, incessant... I clench my teeth.

Faster.

Blue to pink, spark-shot... A catlick of fire... Another ... Heatless flames dance like sea plants... Higher, rising higher... Walls of fire buckle and crackle...

Footfalls at my back.

Don't look. Shift.

Sky split down the middle, by sun a comet streaking... Here and gone... Again. Again. Three days in as many heartbeats... I breathe the air spicy... Swirl the fires, descend to purple earth . . . Prism in the sky . . . I race the course of a glowing river across a field of fungus color of blood, spongy . . . Spores that turn to jewels, fall like bullets . . .

Night on a plain of brass, footfalls echoing to eternity . . . Knobbed machinelike plants clanking, metal flowers retracting back to metal stalks, stalks to consoles . . . Clank, clank, sigh . . . Echoes only, at my back?

I spin once.

Was that a dark figure ducking behind a windmill tree? Or only the dance of shadows in my shadow-shifting eyes?

Forward. Through glass and sandpaper, orange ice, landscape of pale flesh . . .

There is no sun, only pale light . . . There is no earth . . . Only thin bridges and islands in the air . . . The world is crystal matrix . . .

Up, down, around . . . Through a hole in the air and down a chute . . .

Sliding . . . To a cobalt beach beside a still copper sea . . . Twilight without stars . . . Faint glow everywhere . . . Dead, dead this place . . . Blue rocks . . . Broken statues of inhuman beings . . . Nothing stirring . . .

Stop.

I drew a magic circle about me in the sand and invested it with the forces of Chaos. I spread my new cloak then at its center, stretched out and went to sleep. I dreamed that the waters rose up to wash away a portion of the circle, and that a green, scaly being with purple hair and sharp teeth crept out of the sea and came to me to drink my blood.

When I awoke, I saw that the circle was broken and a green, scaly being with purple hair and sharp teeth lay dead upon the beach a half-dozen yards from me, Frakir knotted tightly about its throat and the sand disturbed all around. I must have slept very deeply.

I retrieved my strangling cord and crossed another bridge over infinity.

* * *

On the next leg of my journey I was nearly caught up in a flash flood the first time I paused to rest. I was no longer unwary, however, and I kept ahead of it long enough to shift away. I received another warning—in burning letters on the face of an obsidian mountain—suggesting I withdraw, retire, go home. My shouted invitation to a conference was ignored.

I traveled till it was time to sleep again, and I camped then in the Blackened Lands—still, gray, musty, and foggy. I found myself an easily defended cleft, warded it against magic and slept.

Later—how much later, I am uncertain—I was awakened from a dreamless slumber by the pulsing of Frakir upon my wrist.

I was instantly awake, and then I wondered why. I heard nothing and I saw nothing untoward within my limited field of vision. But Frakir—who is not 100 percent perfect—always has a reason when she does give an alarm. I waited, and I recalled my image of the Logrus while I did so. When it was fully before me I fitted my hand within it as if it were a glove and I reached . . .

I seldom carry a blade above the length of a middle-sized dagger. It's too damned cumbersome having several feet of steel hanging at my side, bumping into me, catching onto bushes, and occasionally even tripping me up. My father, and most of the others in Amber and the Courts, swear by the heavy, awkward things, but they are probably made of sterner stuff than myself. I've nothing against them in principle. I love fencing, and I've had a lot of training in their use. I just find carrying one all the time to be a nuisance. The belt even rubs a raw place on my hip after a while. Normally, I prefer Frakir and improvisation. However . . .

This, I was willing to admit, might be a good time to be holding one. For now I heard bellowslike hissing sounds and scrambling noises from somewhere outside and to my left.

I extended through Shadow, seeking a blade. I extended, I extended . . .

Damn. I had come far from any metalworking culture of the appropriate anatomy and at the proper phase in its historical development.

I continued to reach, sweat suddenly beading my brow. Far, very far. And the sounds came nearer, louder, faster.

There came rattling, stamping and spitting noises. A roar. Contact!

I felt the haft of the weapon in my hand. Seize and summon! I called it to me, and I was thrown against the wall by the force of its delivery. I hung there a moment before I could draw it from the sheath in which it was still encased. In that moment, things grew silent outside.

I waited ten seconds. Fifteen. Half a minute . . .

Nothing now.

I wiped my palms on my trousers. I continued to listen. Finally, I advanced.

There was nothing immediately before the opening save a light fog, and as the peripheral lines of sight opened there was still nothing to behold.

Another step . . .

No.

Another.

I was right at the threshold now. I leaned forward and darted a quick glance in either direction.

Yes. There was something off to the left—dark, low, unmoving, half masked by the fog. Crouched? Ready to spring at me?

Whatever it was, it did not stir and it kept total silence. I did the same. After a time, I noticed another dark form of the same general outline beyond it—and possibly a third even farther away. None of them showed any inclination to raise the sort of hell I had been listening to but minutes before.

I continued my vigil.

Several minutes must have passed before I stepped outside. Nothing was roused by my movement. I took another step and waited. Then another.

Finally, moving slowly, I approached the first form. An

ugly brute, covered with scales the color of dried blood. A couple of hundred pounds' worth of creature, long and sinuous . . . Nasty teeth, too, I noted, when I opened its mouth with the point of my weapon. I knew it was safe to do this, because its head was almost completely severed from the rest of it. A very clean cut. A yellow-orange liquid still flowed from the wound.

And I could see from where I stood that the other two forms were creatures of the same sort. In all ways. They were dead, too. The second one I examined had been run through several times and was missing one leg. The third had been hacked to pieces. All of them oozed, and they smelled faintly of cloves.

I inspected the well-trampled area. Mixed in with that strange blood and the dew were what seemed to be the partial impressions of a boot, human-scale. I sought farther and I came across one intact footprint. It was pointed back in the direction from which I had come.

My pursuer? S, perhaps? The one who had called off the dogs? Coming to my aid?

I shook my head. I was tired of looking for sense where there wasn't any. I continued to search, but there were no more full tracks. I returned to the cleft then and picked up my blade's sheathe. I fitted the weapon into it and hung it from my belt. I fastened it over my shoulders so that it hung down my back. The hilt would protrude just above my backpack once I'd shouldered that item. I couldn't see how I could jog with it at my side.

I ate some bread and the rest of the meat. Drank some water, too, and a mouthful of wine. I resumed my journey.

I ran much of the next day—though "day" is something of a misnomer beneath unchanging stippled skies, checkered skies, skies lit by perpetual pinwheels and fountains of light. I ran until I was tired, and I rested and ate and ran some more. I rationed my food, for I'd a feeling I'd have to send far for more and such an act places its own energy demands upon the body. I eschewed shortcuts, for flashy shadows-spanning hellruns also have their price and I did not want to be all whacked out when I arrived. I checked behind me often. Usually, I saw nothing suspicious. Occasionally, though, I thought that I glimpsed distant pursuit. Other explanations were possible, however, considering some of the tricks the shadows can play.

I ran until I knew that I was finally nearing my destination. There came no new disaster followed by an order to turn back. I wondered fleetingly whether this was a good sign, or if the worst were yet to come. Either way, I knew that one more sleep and a little more journeying would put me where I wanted to be. Add a little caution and a few precautions and there might even be reason for optimism.

I ran through a vast, forestlike stand of crystalline shapes. Whether they were truly living things or represented some geological phenomenon, I did not know. They distorted perspectives and made shifting difficult. However, I saw no signs of living things in that glossy, glassy place, which led me to consider making my final campsite there.

I broke off a number of the limbs and drove them into the pink ground, which had the consistency of partly set putty. I constructed a circular palisade standing to about shoulder-height, myself at its center. I unwound Frakir from my wrist then voiced the necessary instructions as I placed her atop my rough and shining wall.

Frakir elongated, stretching herself as thin as a thread and twining among the shardlike branches. I felt safe. I did not believe anything could cross that barrier without Frakir's springing loose and twining herself to deathly tightness about it.

I spread my cloak, lay down, and slept. For how long, I am not certain. And I recall no dreams. There were no disturbances either.

When I woke I moved my head to reorient it, but the view was the same. In every direction but down the view was filled with interwoven crystal branches. I climbed slowly to my feet and pressed against them. Solid. They had become a glass cage.

Although I was able to break off some lesser branches, these were mainly from overhead, and it did nothing to work my release. Those which I had planted initially had thickened considerably, having apparently rooted themselves solidly. They would not yield to my strongest kicks.

The damned thing infuriated me. I swung my blade and glassy chips flew all about. I muffled my face with my cloak then and swung several times more. Then I noticed that my hand felt wet. When I looked at it, I saw that it was running with blood. Some of those splinters were very sharp. I desisted with the blade and returned to kicking at my enclosure. The walls creaked occasionally and made chiming noises, but they held.

I am not normally claustrophobic and my life was not in imminent peril, but something about this shining prison annoyed me out of all proportion to the situation itself. I raged for perhaps ten minutes before I forced myself to sufficient calmness that I might think clearly.

I studied the tangle until I discerned the uniform color and texture of Frakir running through it. I placed my fingertips upon her and spoke an order. Her brightness increased and she ran through the spectrum and settled into a red glow. The first creaking sound occurred a few seconds later.

I quickly withdrew to the center of the enclosure and wrapped myself fully in my cloak. If I crouched, I decided, some of the overhead pieces would fall a greater distance, striking me with more force. So I stood upright, protecting my head and neck with my arms and hands as well as with the cloak.

The creaking sounds became cracking sounds, followed by rattling, snapping, breaking. I was suddenly struck across the shoulder, but I maintained my footing.

Ringing and crunching, the edifice began to fall about me. I held my ground, though I was struck several times more.

When the sounds ceased and I looked again I saw that the roof had been removed, and I stood calf-deep amid fallen branches of the hard, corallike material. Several of the side members had splintered off at near to ground level. Others now stood at unnatural angles, and this time a few well-placed kicks brought them down.

My cloak was torn in a number of places, and Frakir coiled now about my left ankle and began to migrate to my wrist. The stuff crunched underfoot as I departed.

I shook out my cloak and brushed myself off. I traveled for perhaps half an hour then, leaving the place far behind me, before I halted and took my breakfast in a hot, bleak valley smelling faintly of sulfur.

As I was finishing, I heard a crashing noise. A horned and tusked purple thing went racing along the ridge to my right pursued by a hairless orange-skinned creature with long claws and a forked tail. Both were wailing in different keys.

I nodded. It was just one damned thing after another.

I made my way through frozen lands and burning lands, under skies both wild and placid. Then at last, hours later, I saw the low range of dark hills, and aurora streaming upward from behind them. That was it. I needed but approach and pass through and I would see my goal beyond the last and most difficult barrier of all.

I moved ahead. It would be good to finish this job and get on with more important matters. I would trump back to Amber when I was finished there, rather than retracing my steps. I could not have trumped in to my destination, though, because the place could not be represented on a card.

In that I was jogging, I first thought that the vibrations were my own. I was disabused of this notion when small pebbles began to roll aimlessly about the ground before me.

Why not?

I'd been hit with just about everything else. It was as if my strange nemesis were working down through a checklist and had just now come to "Earthquake." All right. At least there was nothing high near at hand to fall on me.

"Enjoy yourself, you son of a bitch!" I called out. "One day real soon it won't be so funny!"

As if in response the shaking grew more violent, and I

had to halt or be thrown from my feet. As I watched, the ground began to subside in places, tilt in still others. I looked about quickly, trying to decide whether to advance, retreat, or stay put. Small fissures had begun to open, and now I could hear a growling, grinding sound.

The earth dropped abruptly beneath me—perhaps six inches—and the nearest crevices widened. I turned and began sprinting back the way I had come. The ground seemed less disturbed there.

A mistake perhaps. A particularly violent tremor followed, knocking me from my feet. Before I could rise a large crack appeared within reaching distance. It continued to widen even as I watched. I sprang to my feet, leapt across it, stumbled, rose again, and beheld another opening rift— widening more rapidly than the one I had been fleeing.

I sprang once more, onto a tilting tabletop of land. The ground seemed torn everywhere now with the dark lightning strokes of rifts, heaving themselves open widely to the accompaniment of awful groans and screechings. Big sections of ground slipped from sight into abysses. My small island was already going.

I leaped again, and again, trying to make it over to what appeared to be a more stable area.

I didn't quite manage it. I missed my footing and fell. But I managed to catch hold of the edge. I dangled a moment then and began to draw myself upward. The edge began to crumble. I clawed at it and caught a fresh hold. Then I dangled again, coughing and cursing.

I sought for footholds in the clayey wall against which I hung. It yielded somewhat beneath the thrusting of my boots and I dug in, blinking dirt from my eyes, trying for a firmer hold overhead. I could feel Frakir loosening, tightening into a small loop, one end free and flowing over my knuckles, hopefully to locate something sufficiently firm-set to serve as an anchor.

But no. My lefthand hold gave way again. I clung with my right and groped for another. Loose earth fell about me as I failed, and my right hand was beginning to slip.

Dark shadow above me, through dust and swimming eyes.

My right hand fell loose. I thrust with my legs for another try.

My right wrist was clasped as it sped upward and forward once again. A big hand with a powerful grip held me. Moments later, it was joined by another and I was drawn upward, quickly, smoothly. I was over the edge and seeking my footing in an instant. My wrist was released. I wiped my eyes.

"Luke!"

He was dressed in green, and blades must not have bothered him the way they do me, for a good-sized one hung at his right side. He seemed to be using a rolled cloak for a backpack, and he wore its clasp like a decoration upon his left breast—an elaborate thing, a golden bird of some sort.

"This way," he said, turning, and I followed him.

He led me a course back and to the left, tangent to the route I had taken on entering the valley. The footing grew steadier as we hurried that way, mounting at last a low hill that seemed completely out of range in the disturbance. Here we paused to look back.

"Come no farther!" a great voice boomed from that direction.

"Thanks, Luke," I panted. "I don't know how you're here or why but—"

He raised a hand. "Right now I just want to know one thing," he said, rubbing at a short beard he seemed to have grown in an amazingly brief time, and causing me to note that he was wearing the ring with the blue stone.

"Name it," I told him.

"How come whatever it was that just spoke has your voice?" he asked.

"Uh-oh. I knew it sounded familiar."

"Come on!" he said. "You must know. Every time you're threatened and it warns you back it's your voice that I hear doing it—echolike."

"How long have you been following me, anyhow?"

"Quite a distance."

"Those dead creatures outside the cleft where I'd camped—"

"I took them out for you. Where are you going, and what is that thing?"

"Right now I have only suspicions as to exactly what's going on, and it's a long story. But the answer should lie beyond that next range of hills."

I gestured toward the aurora.

He stared off in that direction, then nodded.

"Let's get going," he said.

"There is an earthquake in progress," I observed.

"It seems pretty much confined to this valley," he stated. "We can cut around it and proceed."

"And quite possibly encounter its continuance."

He shook his head. "It seems to me," he said, "that whatever it is that's trying to bar your way exhausts itself after each effort and takes quite a while to recover sufficiently to make another attempt."

"But the attempts are getting closer together," I noted, "and more spectacular each time."

"Is it because we're getting closer to their source?" he asked.

"Possibly."

"Then let's hurry."

We descended the far side of the hill, then went up and down another. The tremors, by that time, had already subsided to an occasional shuddering of the ground and shortly these, too, ceased.

We made our way into and along another valley, which for a while headed us far to the right of our goal, then curved gently back in the proper direction, toward the final range of barren hills, lights flickering beyond them against the low, unmoving base of a cloudlike line of white under a mauve to violet sky. No fresh perils were presented.

"Luke," I asked after a time, "what happened on the mountain, that night in New Mexico?"

"I had to go away—fast," he answered.

"What about Dan Martinez's body?"

"Took it with me."

"Why?"

"I don't like leaving evidence lying about."

"That doesn't really explain much."

"I know," he said, and he broke into a jog.

I paced him.

"And you know who I am," I continued.

"Yes."

"How?"

"Not now," he said. "Not now."

He increased his pace. I matched it.

"And why were you following me?"

"I saved your ass, didn't I?"

"Yeah, and I'm grateful. But it still doesn't answer the question."

"Race you to that leaning stone," he said, and he put on a burst of speed.

I did, too, and I caught him. Try as I could I couldn't pass him, though. And we were breathing too hard by then to ask or answer questions.

I pushed myself, ran faster. He did, too, keeping up. The leaning stone was still a good distance off. We stayed side by side and I saved my reserve for the final sprint. It was crazy, but I'd run against him too many times. It was almost a matter of habit by now. That, and the old curiosity. Had he gotten a little faster? Had I? Or a little slower?

My arms pumped, my feet thudded. I got control of my breathing, maintained it in an appropriate rhythm. I edged a little ahead of him and he did nothing about it. The stone was suddenly a lot nearer.

We held our distance for perhaps half a minute, and then he cut loose. He was abreast of me, he was past me. Time to dig in.

I drove my legs faster. The blood thudded in my ears. I sucked air and pushed with everything I had. The distance between us began to narrow again. The leaning rock was looking bigger and bigger...

I caught him before we reached it, but try as I might I could not pull ahead. We raced past it side by side and collapsed together.

"Photo finish," I gasped.

"Got to call it a tie," he paused. "You always surprise me—right at the end."

I groped out my water bottle and passed it to him. He took a swig and handed it back. We emptied it that way, a little at a time.

"Damn," he said then, getting slowly to his feet. "Let's see what's over those hills."

I got up and went along.

When I finally recovered my breath the first thing I said was, "You seem to know a hell of a lot more about me than I do about you."

"I think so," he said after a long pause, "and I wish I didn't."

"What does that mean?"

"Not now," he replied. "Later. You don't read *War and Peace* on your coffee break."

"I don't understand."

"Time," he said. "There's always either too much time or not enough. Right now there's not enough."

"You've lost me."

"Wish I could."

The hills were nearer and the ground remained firm beneath our feet. We trudged steadily onward.

I thought of Bill's guesswork, Random's suspicions, and Meg Devlin's warning. I also thought of that round of strange ammunition I'd found in Luke's jacket.

"That thing we're heading toward," he said, before I could frame a fresh question of my own. "That's your Ghostwheel, isn't it?"

"Yes."

He laughed. Then: "So you were telling the truth back in Santa Fe when you told me it required a peculiar environment. What you didn't say was that you'd found that environment and built the thing there."

I nodded. "What about your plans for a company?" I asked him.

"That was just to get you to talk about it."

"And what about Dan Martinez—the things he said?"

"I don't know. I really didn't know him. I still don't know what he wanted, or why he came at us shooting."

"Luke, what is it that you want, anyhow?"

"Right now I just want to see that damned thing," he said. "Did building it out here in the boonies endow it with some sort of special properties?"

"Yes."

"Like what?"

"Like a few I didn't even think of—unfortunately," I answered.

"Name one."

"Sorry," I said. "Question and answer is a two-way game."

"Hey, I'm the guy who just pulled you out of a hole in the ground."

"I gather you're also the guy who tried to kill me on a bunch of April thirtieths."

"Not recently," he said. "Honest."

"You mean you really did?"

"Well . . . yeah. But I had reasons. It's a long story and—"

"Jesus, Luke! Why? What did I ever do to you?"

"It's not that simple," he answered.

We reached the base of the nearest hill and he started climbing it.

"Don't," I called to him. "You can't go over."

He halted. "Why not?"

"The atmosphere ends thirty or forty feet up."

"You're kidding."

I shook my head.

"And it's worse on the other side," I added. "We have to find a passage through. There's one farther to the left."

I turned and headed in that direction. Shortly, I heard his footfalls.

"So you gave it your voice," he said.

"So?"

"So I see what you're up to and what's been going on. It's become sentient in that crazy place you built it. It went wild, and you're heading to shut it down. It knows it and it's got the power to do something about it. It's your Ghostwheel that's been trying to get you to turn back, isn't it?"

"Probably."

"Why didn't you just trump in?"

"You can't construct a Trump for a place that keeps changing. What do you know about Trumps, anyway?"

"Enough," he said.

I saw the passage I was seeking up ahead.

I approached the place and I halted before I entered it.

"Luke," I said, "I don't know what you want or why or how you got here, and you don't seem to care to tell me. I will tell you something for free, though. This could be very dangerous. Maybe you ought to go back to wherever you came from and let me handle it. There's no reason to place you in jeopardy."

"I think there is," he said. "Besides, I might be useful."

"How?"

He shrugged. "Let's get on with it, Merlin. I want to see that thing."

"Okay. Come on."

I led the way into the narrow place where the stone had been riven.

CHAPTER 10

The passage was long and dark and occasionally tight, growing progressively colder as we advanced, but at length we emerged onto the wide, rocky shelf that faced the steaming pit. There was an ammonialike odor in the air, and my feet were cold and my face flushed, as usual. I blinked hard several times, studying the latest outlines of the maze through the shifting mist. A pearl-gray pall hung over the entire area. Intermittent orange flashes penetrated the gloom.

"Uh—where is it?" Luke inquired.

I gestured straight ahead, toward the site of the latest flicker. "Out there," I told him.

Just then, the mists were swept away, revealing file upon file of dark, smooth ridges separated by black declivities. The ridges zigged and zagged their way out toward a fortresslike island, a low wall running about it, several metallic structures visible beyond.

"It's a—maze," he remarked. "Do we travel it down in the passages or up on top of the walls?"

I smiled as he studied it.

"It varies," I said. "Sometimes up and sometimes down."

"Well, which way do we go?"

"I don't know yet. I have to study it each time. You see, it keeps changing, and there's a trick to it."

"A trick?"

"More than one, actually. The whole damn thing is floating on a lake of liquid hydrogen and helium. The maze moves around. It's different each time. And then there's a matter of the atmosphere. If you were to walk upright along the ridges you would be above it in most places. You wouldn't last long. And the temperature ranges from horribly cold to roasting hot over a range of a few feet in elevation. You have to know when to crawl and when to climb and when to do other things—as well as which way to go."

"How do you tell?"

"Un-uh," I said. "I'll take you in, but I'm not giving you the secret."

The mists began to rise again from the depths and to collect into small clouds.

"I see now why you can't make a Trump for it," he began.

I continued to study the layout.

"All right," I said then. "This way."

"What if it attacks us while we're in the maze?" he asked.

"You can stay behind if you want."

"No. Are you really going to shut it down?"

"I'm not sure. Come on."

I took several steps ahead and to the right. A faint circle of light appeared in the air before me, grew brighter. I felt Luke's hand upon my shoulder.

"What—?" he began.

"No farther!" the voice I now recognized as my own said to me.

"I think we can work something out," I responded. "I have several ideas and—"

"No!" it answered. "I heard what Random said."

"I am prepared to disregard his order," I said, "if there is a better alternative."

"You're trying to trick me. You want to shut me down."

"You're making things worse with all these power displays," I said. "I'm coming in now and—"

"No!"

A heavy gust of wind blew out of the circle and struck against me. I was staggered by it. I saw my sleeve turn brown, then orange. It began to fray even as I watched.

"What are you doing? I have to talk to you, explain—"

"Not here! Not now! Never!"

I was hurled back against Luke, who caught me, dropping to one knee as he did so. An arctic blast assailed us and icy crystals danced before my eyes. Bright colors began to flash then, half blinding me.

"Stop!" I cried, but nothing did.

The ground seemed to tilt beneath us and suddenly there was no ground. It did not feel as if we were falling, however. It seemed rather as if we hung suspended in the midst of a blizzard of light.

"Stop!" I called out once again, but the words were swept away.

The circle of light vanished, as if retreating down a long tunnel. I realized, however, through the sensory overload, that it was Luke and I who were receding from the light, that we had already been blasted a great enough distance to drive us halfway through the hill. But there was nothing solid in any direction about us.

A faint buzzing sound began. It grew into a humming, then a dull roar. In the distance, I seemed to see a tiny steam locomotive negotiating a mountainside at an impossible angle, then an upside-down waterfall, a skyline beneath green waters. A park bench passed us quickly, a blue-skinned woman seated upon it, clutching at it, a horrified expression on her face.

I dug frantically within my pocket, knowing we might be destroyed at any moment.

"What," Luke screamed into my ear, his grip now almost dislocating my arm, "is it?"

"Shadow-storm!" I cried back. "Hang on!" I added unnecessarily.

A batlike creature was blown into my face, was gone an instant later, leaving a wet slash upon my right cheek. Something struck against my left foot.

An inverted mountain range flowed past us, buckling and rippling. The roaring increased in volume. The light seemed to pulse by us now, in wide bands of color, touching us with a near-physical force. Heat lamps and wind chimes . . .

I heard Luke cry out as if he had been struck, but I was unable to turn to his aid. We traversed a region of lightninglike flashes where my hair stood on end and my skin tingled.

I gripped the packet of cards within my pocket and withdrew it. At this point we were beginning to spin and I was afraid they would be torn from my hand. I held them tightly, fearing to sort through them, keeping them close to my body. I drew them upward slowly, carefully. Whichever one lay on top would have to be our exit.

Dark bubbles formed and broke about us, discharging noxious fumes.

I saw, as I raised my hand, that my skin was gray in appearance, sparkling with fluorescent swirls. Luke's hand upon my arm looked cadaverous, and when I glanced back at him a grinning death's head met my gaze.

I looked away, turned my attention back to the cards. It was hard to focus my vision, through the grayness, through a peculiar distancing effect. But it finally came clear. It was the grassy spit of land I had regarded—how long ago?— quiet waters about it, the edge of something crystalline and bright jutting into view off toward the right.

I held it within my attention. Sounds from beyond my shoulder indicated that Luke was trying to address me, but I could not distinguish his words. I continued to regard the Trump and it grew clearer. But slowly, slowly. Something struck me hard, below the right side of my rib cage. I forced myself to ignore it and continued to concentrate.

At last the scene on the card seemed to move toward me, to grow larger. There was a familiar sense of coldness to it now as the scene engulfed me and I it. An almost elegiac feeling of stillness hung over that little lake.

I fell forward into the grass, my heart pounding, my side throbbing. I was gasping, and the subjective sense of worlds rushing by me was still present, like the afterimages of highways upon closing one's eyes at the end of a long day's drive.

Smelling sweet water, I passed out.

I was vaguely aware of being dragged, carried, then helped, stumbling along. There followed a spell of full unconsciousness, shading over into sleep and dreaming.

. . . I walked the streets of a ruined Amber beneath a lowering sky. A crippled angel with a fiery sword stalked the heights above me, slashing. Wherever its blade fell, smoke, dust, and flame rose up. Its halo was my Ghostwheel, pouring forth mighty winds ridden by abominations that streamed past the angel's face like a dark, living veil, working disorder and ruin wherever they fell. The palace was half collapsed, and there were gibbets nearby where my relatives hung, twisting in the gusts. I'd a blade in one hand and Frakir dangled from the other. I was climbing now, going up to meet and do battle with the bright-dark nemesis. An awful feeling lay upon me as I mounted my rocky way, as if my imminent failure was a thing foregone. Even so, I decided, the creature was going to leave here with wounds to lick.

It took note of me as I drew near, turning in my direction. Its face was still hidden as it raised its weapon. I rushed forward, regretting only that I had not had time to envenom my blade. I spun twice as I went in, feinting, to strike somewhere in the vicinity of its left knee.

There followed a flash of light and I was falling, falling, bits of flame descending about me, like a burning blizzard.

I fell so for what seemed an age and a half, coming to rest at last upon my back atop a large stone table marked out like a sundial, its stylus barely missing impaling me— which seemed crazy even in a dream. There were no sundials in the Courts of Chaos, for there is no sun there. I was located at the edge of a courtyard beside a high, dark tower, and I found myself unable to move, let alone rise. Above me, my mother, Dara, stood upon a low balcony in her natural form, looking down at me in her awful power and beauty.

"Mother!" I cried. "Free me!"

"I have sent one to help you," she answered.

"And what of Amber?"

"I do not know."

"And my father?"

"Speak not to me of the dead."

The stylus turned slowly, positioned itself above my throat, began a gradual but steady descent.

"Help me!" I cried. "Hurry!"

"Where are you?" she called out, head turning, eyes darting. "Where have you gone?"

"I'm still here!" I yelled.

"Where are you?"

I felt the stylus touch the side of my neck—

The vision broke and fell apart.

My shoulders were propped against something unyielding, my legs were stretched out before me. Someone had just squeezed my shoulder, the hand brushing against my neck.

"Merle, you okay? Want a drink?" a familiar voice was asking.

I took a deep breath and sighed it out. I blinked several times. The light was blue, the world a field of lines and angles. A dipper of water appeared before my mouth.

"Here." It was Luke's voice.

I drank it all.

"Want another?"

"Yes."

"Just a minute."

I felt his weight shift, heard his footsteps recede. I regarded the diffusely illuminated wall six or seven feet before me.

I ran my hand along the floor. It seemed to be of the same material.

Shortly, Luke returned, smiling, and passed me the dipper. I drained it and handed it back.

"Want more?" he asked.

"No. Where are we?"

"In a cave—a big, pretty place."

"Where'd you get the water?"

"In a side cavern, up that way." He gestured. "Several barrels of it in there. Also lots of food. Want something to eat?"

"Not yet. Are you okay?"

"Kind of beat," he replied, "but intact. You don't seem to have any broken bones, and that cut on your face has stopped bleeding."

"That's something, anyway," I said.

I climbed slowly to my feet, the final strands of dreams withdrawing slowly as I rose. I saw then that Luke had turned and was walking away. I followed him for several paces before I thought to inquire, "Where are you going?"

"In there," he answered, pointing with the dipper.

I followed him through an opening in the wall and into a cold cavern about the size of my old apartment's living room. Four large wooden barrels stood along the wall to my left, and Luke proceeded to hang the dipper upon the upper edge of the nearest. Against the far wall were great stacks of cartons and piles of sacks.

"Canned goods," he announced. "Fruit, vegetables, ham, salmon, biscuits, sweets. Several cases of wine. A Coleman stove. Plenty of Sterno. Even a bottle or two of cognac."

He turned and brushed quickly past me, headed on up the hall again.

"Now where?" I asked.

But he was moving fast and did not reply. I had to hurry to catch up. We passed several branches and openings before he halted at another, nodding.

"Latrine in there. Just a hole with some boards over it. Good idea to keep it covered, I'd say."

"What the hell is this?" I asked.

He raised his hand. "It will all become clear in a minute. This way."

He swung around a sapphire corner and vanished. Almost completely disoriented, I moved in that direction. After several turns and one cutback, I felt totally lost. Luke was nowhere in sight.

I halted and listened. Not a sound except for my own breathing.

"Luke! Where are you?" I called.

"Up here," he answered.

The voice seemed to be coming from overhead and somewhere off to my right. I ducked beneath a low arch and came into a bright blue chamber of the same crystalline substance as the rest of the place. I saw a sleeping bag and a pillow in one corner. Light streamed in from a small opening about eight feet overhead.

"Luke?" I asked again.

"Here," came his reply.

I moved to position myself beneath the hole, squinting against the brightness as I stared upward. Finally, I shaded my eyes. Luke's head and shoulders was limned above me, his hair a crown of coppery flame in what could be the light of early morning or of evening. He was smiling again.

"That, I take it, is the way out," I said.

"For me," he answered.

"What do you mean?"

There followed a grating noise and the view was partly occluded by the edge of a large boulder.

"What are you doing?"

"Moving this stone into a position where I can block the opening quickly," he replied, "and stick in a few wedges afterward."

"Why?"

"There are sufficient tiny openings for air so that you shan't suffocate," he went on.

"Great. Why am I here, anyway?"

"Let's not get existential just now," he said. "This isn't a philosophy seminar."

"Luke! Damn it! What's going on?"

"It should be obvious that I'm making you a prisoner," he said. "The blue crystal, by the way, will block any Trump sendings and negate your magical abilities that rely on things beyond the walls. I need you alive and fangless for now, in a place where I can get to you in a hurry."

I studied the opening and the nearby walls.

"Don't try it," he said. "I have the advantage of position."

"Don't you think you owe me an explanation?"

He stared at me for a moment, then nodded.

"I have to go back," he said finally, "and try to get control of the Ghostwheel. Any suggestions?"

I laughed. "It's not on the best of terms with me at the moment. I'm afraid I can't help you."

He nodded again. "I'll just have to see what I can do. God, what a weapon! If I can't swing it myself I'll have to come back and pick your brains for some ideas. You be thinking about it, okay?"

"I'll be thinking about a lot of things, Luke. You're not going to like some of them."

"You're not in a position to do much."

"Not yet," I said.

He caught hold of the boulder, began to move it.

"Luke!" I cried.

He paused, studied me, his expression changing to one I had never seen before.

"That's not really my name," he stated, after a moment.

"What, then?"

"I am your cousin Rinaldo," he said slowly. "I killed Caine, and I came close with Bleys. I missed with the bomb at the funeral, though. Someone spotted me. I will destroy the House of Amber with or without your Ghostwheel— but it would make things a lot easier if I had that kind of power."

"What's your bitch, Luke?... Rinaldo? Why the vendetta?"

"I went after Caine first," he continued, "because he's the one who actually killed my father."

"I—didn't know." I stared at the flash of the Phoenix clasp upon his breast. "I didn't know that Brand had a son," I finally said.

"You do now, old buddy. That's another reason why I can't let you go, and why I have to keep you in a place like this. Don't want you warning the others."

"You're not going to be able to pull this off."

He was silent for several seconds, then he shrugged.

"Win or lose, I have to try."

"Why April 30?" I said suddenly. "Tell me that."

"It was the day I got the news of my dad's death."

He drew upon the boulder and it slid into the hole, blocking it fully. There followed some brief hammerings.

"Luke!"

He did not answer. I could see his shadow through the translucent stone. After a while it straightened, then dropped from sight. I heard his boots strike the ground outside.

"Rinaldo!"

He did not answer and I heard his retreating footsteps.

I count the days by the lightening and darkening of the blue crystal walls. It has been over a month since my imprisonment, though I do not know how slowly or rapidly time flows here in relation to other shadows. I have paced every hall and chamber of this great cave, but I have found no way out. My Trumps do not work here, not even the Trumps of Doom. My magic is useless to me, limited as it is by walls the color of Luke's ring. I begin to feel that I might enjoy even the escape of temporary insanity, but my reason refuses to surrender to it, there being too many puzzles to trouble me: Dan Martinez, Meg Devlin, my Lady of the Lake. Why? And why did he spend all of that time in my company. Luke. Rinaldo, my enemy? I have to find a way to warn the others. If he succeeds in ruining Ghostwheel them then Brand's dream—my nightmare of conquest—will be realized. I see now that I have made many mistakes . . . Forgive me, Julia . . . I will pace the measure of my confinement yet again. Somewhere there must be a gap in the icy blue logic that surrounds me, against which I hurl my mind, my cries, my bitter laughter. Up this hall, down the tunnel. The blue is everywhere. The shadows will not bear me away, for there are no shadows here. I am Merlin the pent, son of Corwin the lost, and my dream of light has been turned against me. I stalk my prison like my own ghost. I cannot let it end this way. Perhaps the next tunnel, or the next . . .